Merlin and the Moor

The Saga Begins

Reina Donovan

Table of Contents

Prologue: Merlin's Escape

Monstrous fires blazed around Merlin as he tore through what remained of the forest, the fires threatening to swallow him whole.

It was the dead of night, but the orange light burned for miles, illuminating his path. His skin was covered in a thin layer of sweat and soot, and he had tiny little slashes as low branches cut his flesh when he ran straight through them.

Keep going, he told himself. *You are almost there. Just a little bit further.*

He could almost hear the manic laugh of the Djinn ringing in his ears, which was enough motivation to keep his pace fast and steady. His lungs burned, and his muscles were aching to the point where he was certain he had torn a ligament, but his momentum did not waver. A few hours, days, or even weeks of pain was well worth it if it meant escaping a lifetime of torture from the Djinn's hand.

Leaping over the familiar stack of rocks, Merlin knew he was close to home. With the fires nipping at his heels, the light made the tan canvas of his tent visible, even in the dense forest. There would be nothing left of it by morning. None of that mattered though; if he did not leave now, the fate of magic and mankind would be sealed.

Reaching the end of his journey, Merlin came to a skidded halt, whipping past the flap of the tent and grabbing the first sack he could find. He had been grateful that the Djinn's wrath had not reached this part of the forest, and that his precious belongings remained untouched—not that most of the things in his tent held any real sentimental value. They were mere tokens of his travels and possessions that he had collected from the places he had gone in his lifetime. None of them would serve any real importance where he was going, except for one.

Casting his thin bedroll aside, Merlin dropped to his knees and furiously dug at the exposed earth with his bare hands. Damp dirt caked on his fingertips within seconds. He would have had more luck using a shovel, a spoon, or anything but his hands to unearth the only relic in his home worth saving, but he could not be bothered to look. Time was of the essence, time was everything, and time would be what saved them all.

It was then that he found it—the small wooden box he had buried when he first made camp out in the forest. It was not easy to pry from the earth, but once he had gotten his fingers around the side, he used whatever strength he had left and yanked it free.

Gulping in a few short breaths, he removed the key from his neck and turned it in the key hole until he heard a quiet click. The lid lifted as if enchanted by magic, and inside sat an ancient relic. Merlin had seen his fair share of magical objects in his mortal life, but none ever so grand as the one in front of him. If mankind knew of its existence or the power it held, he was certain all hell would break loose. There would be wars like no person had ever seen before, all for the possibility of holding the brass contraption that sat in the palm of his hand.

Blood-curdling screams echoed in the distance, bringing Merlin back to reality—the one he was desperate to escape.

The Templars. Merlin's heart ached. They were the noblest, bravest, and wisest order that Merlin had ever come to know. Their mission and legacy were similar to his own; to protect magic in all its forms from the hands of evil. Their greatest enemy, the Djinn, had sought to steal every last artifact in this realm. Over the years, Merlin had tracked down and collected those he could find, to keep them safe.

He came to the crippling realization that their efforts had been futile—they had led the wicked man straight to them.

The cries of his people still rang in the distance. He had little time left to gather what he could. Gripping his traveling device in his right hand, not daring to put it down for a single second, he tore through what remained of his belongings, separating the mementos from the relics he had strategically placed in plain sight.

The second his hand brushed against them, their true form returned, no longer appearing as chipped clay pots or weathered notebooks.

Merlin had learned that some of the lesser relics could be manipulated. It had something to do with the power they held, but nothing outweighed the one in his hands, nor the one the Templars were trying to get to him.

Listening more carefully, he realized that the screams had been silenced. Only the sounds of raging fires crackled in the night.

Just as he tucked the last of his possessions into the leather sack and slung it over his shoulders, a young man barreled into his tent. At first, Merlin feared it had been the Djinn himself, but recognizing the robes and the insignia over the breast, he sighed with relief. One of the Templars had made it.

"Aylwin," Merlin breathed, recognizing the man.

He was of average height, but had a strong build, which was concealed beneath his ropes and subtle pieces of armor. His hair, like most of the Templars, was cut short, exposing the delicate tattoos on his head.

"Merlin." Aylwin saluted. "I feared I would not make it in time."

Untying the leather vest around his chest, the Templar removed an ancient sword from its sheath.

Excalibur. In the flesh.

"You have done the realm the highest honor in bringing it to me on this unholy night," Merlin said quietly, squeezing the Templar's hand to show his sincerest gratitude.

The mighty sword was the only reason that Merlin had waited so long. It was also the reason why many great and honorable men had died that night, trying to get it to him. All of their effort to keep it from the Djinn's hands had been successful.

Merlin's hands had barely grasped the hilt of the magical sword when the tip of a blade suddenly protruded from Aylwin's chest. The Templar coughed and blood splattered onto Merlin's face, chest, and arms. He looked down at the blade until it was ripped out, and the man dropped to his knees before falling face-first onto the dirt.

In his place stood Merlin's greatest enemy, grinning from ear to ear, as he wiped the blood of the last living Templar on the sleeve of his tunic.

"Merlin," he teased. "Did you really think you could outrun *me?*"

"I did not think it, I knew it," Merlin snapped back. "Had I not, I wouldn't be standing here now."

The Djinn's dark eyes flickered at the insult and he lunged in retaliation. Merlin, anticipating the move, was quick to dodge the ill-attempted attack, making sure that his back was never turned to an enemy. They circled the middle of the tent for a few paces, carefully stepping one foot over the other until they stopped to face each other head-on once more.

"I will only say this once," the Djinn seethed. "Hand over the sword, and I'll spare your life."

"No," Merlin said quickly. "The Templars gave their life to see it in my hands. I'm not about to dishonor their sacrifice by giving it up."

"Then you shall die alongside them," the Djinn growled.

This is it. The choice that will change the realm forever.

The Djinn brandished his sword once more, preparing to deliver the final blow and end Merlin's life forever. Just as he did so, Merlin pricked his finger on the traveling relic in his hands. A drop of blood seeped into the device, and picturing the place he wanted to go, a bright light illuminated the entire tent. In the blink of an eye, he—and most importantly, Excalibur—vanished into thin air.

He did not simply travel to a new place in the realm that Merlin had grown up in. No, the device took him through time, and just as easily as he took a breath, he reappeared in a lush forest, centuries into the future.

It looked similar to the area he had settled in the last time, only it was not set ablaze and burning to the ground. It was vibrant and full of life. Setting his leather sack on the forest floor, Merlin went to place the sword on top of it, only it was not in his hands.

"What?" he exclaimed.

He twirled around in circles, believing that he must have dropped it, but it was nowhere to be found. He searched the area in the thickets and overgrown bushes, but Excalibur was gone.

"No, I had it with me, there's no way it was left behind," he said, running his fingers through his hair.

The only explanation that Merlin could come up with was that they must have been separated during a blip in time. He frowned, fearing that all the hard work would be for naught if he could not find Excalibur again, but he would not rest until the legendary sword was safe in his grasp once more.

At least it was well out of the Djinn's reach. That thought alone would always be enough for Merlin to keep pushing forward.

Chapter 1:

Token of Truce

Many different hands poked and prodded Prince Jawar of Raimore as his servants dressed him in his ceremonial robes.

He thought that they were going a little overboard with the formal garments, but he knew it was not his place to voice his opinion—at least not on matters such as maintaining appearance. If his mother, Queen Jacia, wanted him to wear a potato sack, their people would dress him as instructed.

"You look displeased, Your Grace."

Usha, Jawar's personal guard who was tasked with following him anywhere and everywhere, stood just beside his bedchamber doors, a grin twisting his lips. He had watched the young prince for many years, since long before he had taken his first steps. He had become a bit of a father figure in his life, not that he would ever give Usha the satisfaction of saying so.

"It just seems a bit much," Jawar admitted.

"It's important for you to look your best," Usha continued. "Lord Hakim might be blood, but he still holds royal status in the kingdom of Raimore. It's customary to wear the house colors as a sign of welcoming."

"If you say so."

A bright blue sash was tied over his left shoulder, contrasting the black of his tunic and trousers underneath. Almost every last outfit he owned had some shade of black and blue incorporated, so that he might always represent Raimore with honor and pride. Even though Jawar was only 13 years old, he had been taught from a young age the importance of being a prince. He had to walk a certain way or else someone might think that he did not have the strength or bravery to one day rule the kingdom. There were duties he had to see to daily, most of which consisted of him merely existing in the shadow of his father, King Umar.

King Umar was a brilliant, beloved king. Jawar witnessed praise and love from their people every time they stepped foot outside of the castle. Even those from low ranks—people who barely had enough grain in their cupboards to feed their children—bowed before him as if he were a mighty god. Jawar felt a bit intimidated by the sheer force of his father's presence; it would be an enormous task to fill his shoes when it was his turn to ascend to the throne. He only hoped that day would not come for a long while.

"Alright, I think we've dragged this process out long enough," Usha sighed.

Upon feeling the *thud* of his signature staff vibrating against the stone floor, the servants backed away from the prince. None gave a single protest, even if they believed that Jawar still needed tending to. They were on a tight schedule, and the king and queen would have Usha's head if it were not heeded with the highest regard.

"Oskar, head for the palace steps and inform His and Her Majesty that the prince is on his way," Usha instructed one of the younger guards.

The boy, who looked no older than Jawar himself, placed a hand over his heart and gave a definitive nod. Seconds later, he sprinted down the hallway, the clang of his armor disappearing with him.

Usha was getting old, so he delegated a lot of the more strenuous tasks to the newer recruits. He had said it was to break them in faster and weed out the ones who did not have what it took to protect the royal family. But Jawar knew the truth. Usha's knee had never truly healed since all those years ago when Raimore and Taviel waged war against each other. The only reason that he had not retired had simply been because he and the prince had an unbreakable bond, and King Umar respected that.

Heading in the direction that the young guard had run only moments before, Jawar and Usha walked side by side, their strides matching each other.

"I'm excited to see my cousins," Jawar admitted.

He tried to hide a playful spark in his eye, knowing that it was not dignified to run around the courtyards anymore. His parents had made that clear when they first told him a few nights ago that Lord Hakim and his family were coming to the royal palace. While they had not divulged the exact reason for his spontaneous visit, he knew it was not a social call.

"Remember what your father told you," Usha whispered. "Princes do not play, they rule. It's all fine and well to dine and walk with your cousins through the gardens should the weather permit, but—"

"No playing, no running, no laughing, no smiling, and no having fun," Jawar interrupted. While he laughed it off, there was a sting in his words, one that he hoped Usha did not pick up on.

They stopped just outside the main doors of the castle. Usha adjusted Jawar's sash so that it sat properly over his chest and then he gave an encouraging nod. "This welcoming ceremony is just a formality to please Lord Hakim, so try not to take it too seriously, little prince."

"I never do," Jawar teased.

With a wave of his staff, the guards stationed at the front entrance opened the double doors simultaneously, and Prince Jawar stepped out with Usha a few paces behind. A massive crowd had gathered at the bottom of the steps, all cheering and clapping as the prince joined his parents. Several royal guards were surrounding them, all familiar faces. Usha stepped in line with the rest, but not before giving Jawar a subtle wink.

"Just in time," Jawar's mother murmured. "The horns of Lord Hakim's company just blew. They should be arriving through the lower city any moment now."

"There are so many people!" Jawar blinked.

He did not understand why so many commoners cared to greet one of the many lords of the land. He assumed it was simply because he was the brother of the king. Although Jawar had only seen his uncle a handful of times in the past few years, he found him to be a bit more robust than his father. It did not matter the time, place, or topic of conversation; somehow, he always managed to talk about war as if it were going to happen again.

"You'll understand more when you're older," his father said, nudging him gently with his shoulder. "Sometimes we have to do things like this to show a unified front. It helps to keep our enemies at bay."

"I understand."

It was a lie, but Jawar did not have the heart to tell King Umar that he thought it was pointless and unnecessary to make his uncle feel so important that they had to halt everything they were doing, just to appease his pride.

The crowd parted as a row of carriages appeared down the main road of the lower town. Jawar counted five in total, as well as many foot soldiers marching in between them and flanking them on either side. The procession took about five minutes in total, as if his uncle were soaking in every second of attention that he could. Finally, after Jawar started to sweat standing under the blazing afternoon sun, the final carriage pulled up to the front of the stairs, which was exactly 56 steps. He had counted them once when he was a little kid.

A guard opened the carriage door, and Lord Hakim stepped out, brandishing the Raimore colors. He wore a black cloak over one shoulder, and a deep blue tunic underneath. Even from a distance, Jawar spotted the thin black crown—it was more like a decorative headpiece—nestled just above his eyebrows. His cousins filtered out of the other carriages, along with several other royal members who Jawar had never met.

After waving to some of the commoners standing closest to the carriages, Hakim ascended the steps leading up to the castle with his sons in tow.

"King Umar, you look well, as usual." Hakim spread his arms wide as if he were going to hug his brother, but he stopped himself. He gave a short bow to Jawar's mother before kissing the top of her gloved hand. "And Queen Jacia, you radiate the grace and beauty of a goddess."

She smiled and nodded her head in thanks. "Welcome, Lord Hakim. It's always a pleasure when you grace us with your presence."

"That indeed," King Umar added. "Brother, you remember Prince Jawar, my son."

His uncle sidestepped so that he stood tall in front of Jawar. He tried to match his stand, and even went as far as to puff his chest out, but he was no match for his uncle. At least not today. Perhaps one day he might, if he continued to train with the soldiers during his free time.

"My, oh, my," Hakim said. "Last I remember you were but a boy. Now I see you've grown into a young man. You've done well with him, Umar."

"He is heir to the throne," his father stated. "As future King of Raimore, I should hope so."

"Speaking of, we have much to discuss and little time to do it. Shall we meet now to discuss Jawar's fate?"

"My fate?" Jawar asked.

His father nodded and motioned for Usha to step forward. Jawar tried to get his father's attention, but he simply ignored his son as if he were not there. "Take Jawar to the throne room. Hakim and I will meet you there."

"Yes, Your Majesty," Usha bowed. "Come now, Prince Jawar, try to keep up," he teased.

His mother excused herself, taking his cousins inside, where he secretly wished he could go too. With a final wave from King Umar, the people of Raimore were dismissed, returning to their duties almost immediately. Usha led the little prince back into the castle where he was grateful to be protected from the heat of the sun. They walked in silence for a few minutes until Jawar mustered up the courage to speak.

"Why do you think I'm meeting with my uncle and father?" he asked. "What did he mean about my fate?"

"I do not know, Your Grace," Usha said.

"Should I be worried?"

"Your father would never do anything that might put you in harm's way. You know that as well as I do. You're not just his blood or his heir. You're his only child and he loves you."

"I suppose you're right."

They resumed their walk of silence until they rounded the corner that led to the throne room. It was one of the conjoining rooms of his father's bedchambers. He used it, and the war council room, many times years ago. Jawar was much younger at the time, but the memories still burned in his mind as if they were from only yesterday. But Raimore had seen peace since then, and everyone hoped to keep it that way.

Usha knocked on the council door twice with the butt of his staff before he and the prince were let in. Umar sat at the head of the long table, with his brother seated on the right. Jawar spotted a few of the royal guards lingering in the shadows, where the candlelight did not reach. Instead of joining the rest of them, Usha stood two paces behind Jawar's chair.

"Is this your first time in the throne room?" Hakim asked. He tilted his head to the side, studying Jawar's every move.

Jawar swallowed the lump in his throat and lifted his chin high. "Of course not, uncle. Father has allowed me to listen in on many discussions over the years. What concerns Raimore concerns me too."

"Excellent. I'm glad you see it that way," Hakim concluded.

"Father, what's this all about? Why am I here?"

"It's a bit complicated," King Umar began. "As you know, things have been a bit unsettled with Taviel for some time now, and there has been talk that it might lead to another war. We cannot allow this to happen. Raimore barely survived the last time, and I fear we will be wiped out if it happens again."

"So what must we do?" Jawar asked. "Have you drafted a peace treaty? Perhaps we can meet with the king and queen and discuss things like civilized people."

"We've already decided what must be done," Hakim interjected. "You will act as a token of truce on behalf of Raimore."

"A token of truce?" Jawar's eyebrows pinched together as he tried to make sense of what his uncle meant. He glanced at his father who, for perhaps the first time in forever, refused to meet his son's gaze.

Hakim rested a hand on Jawar's forearm, pulling his attention back to his words. It would have been perceived as a gentle gesture, had he not gripped him so tight that he would surely find bruises later on.

"The alliance is hanging on by a thread. It's now or never with Taviel, and this is the only solution to both of our kingdom's problems. You will live in Taviel until your 18th birthday as a sign of peace between our two people. You will be protected by King Castilian, so you have nothing to fear."

"I will accompany the young prince," Usha declared. "I assure you, King Umar, I will see that no harm comes to your son."

"No," Hakim growled. "Only Jawar will be going to Taviel. That was part of the deal. We must trust the other half of our alliance, or this will not work."

"You expect him to go to a foreign land by himself?" Usha gasped. "Your Majesty, he is just a boy."

"No," Umar sighed. "He is our future. But we have no future if he does not do this."

"Father, that's five years away from Raimore, away from you and mother!" Jawar shouted. He stood up so fast that his chair fell to the ground, but neither the king nor his brother flinched.

"You will begin your travels in less than a fortnight. Usha, you will see that my son is prepared for the journey before then. Do I make myself clear?"

"Yes, Your Majesty," Usha nodded.

"But—"

"That is the end of discussion, Jawar. You are going, and there is nothing you can do or say that will change our minds. This is your duty as the prince. It's what you've been preparing for your whole life. Now, I suggest you go to greet your cousins and spend the evening in their company before getting your affairs in order in the morning."

This was a battle that Jawar knew in his heart he would never win.

Usha escorted him out of the room without another word. Jawar's only thoughts this morning would be what he and his cousins would do during their visit—not that he would be preparing to leave the only home he had ever known in less than two weeks.

Chapter 2:

The Possibility of War

"Lord Hakim, a moment of your time please."

An older guard stood in the middle of the footpath, his hand resting on the hilt of his sword. Hakim recognized the man instantly as Ivan Thando. His twin brother, Usha, just so happened to be the young prince's personal guard. While Usha suffered greatly during the last war that the kingdom fought, Ivan was fitter than ever. He had to be, given that he was the king's personal guard. It was one thing to chase after a young man who had no real responsibilities to the kingdom yet, and another for Ivan, who had the weight of the whole country on his shoulders. If he failed to protect King Umar, Raimore would fall to ruin. There was no chance that Prince Jawar would be ready to ascend the throne at his age. He still had much to learn about the real world.

"Ivan," Hakim greeted. "What can I do for you?"

Hakim had come out into the royal gardens for an evening stroll. It reminded him of his estate, the one his brother had been so gracious to give after he and his wife were married. They had raised their three children in that home, two of which had accompanied him on the journey to the royal city, while the youngest had remained with his wife to take care of the home.

"His Majesty King Umar has requested your presence immediately. He stated it was a matter of urgency, but requires your confidentiality on the subject."

Ivan stood tall in the footpath, having not moved a muscle. Hakim's eyes flickered to the insignia on his breast pocket—the symbol for House Al Naseem. Something twisted in the pit of his stomach, but he chose to ignore it for the time being.

"That's odd. It's getting rather late in the evening. I would have thought he'd be getting ready to retire for the night. If I'm not mistaken, he mentioned he wished to dine with his wife."

"Yes, they shared a quick meal, but he received word and requires your expertise and knowledge," Ivan revealed.

The only thing that Hakim had more knowledge of than his older brother was the delicacies of warfare. Clearly, this had to do something with Taviel and his son's journey there to take place in a few days.

"Alright," Hakim agreed. "Is he waiting for me in the throne room? Or perhaps in the sitting room of his bedchamber? It wouldn't be the first time."

"No. He's in the war council room. I am to see that you come alone and that no one disturbs you while you are there."

A secret meeting in the war room *and* he was being completely discreet about whatever conversation they are to have? That certainly piqued Hakim's interest. He waved his hand toward Ivan, a signal to lead the way. He knew that he was going to accompany him to the door regardless, so he may as well be properly escorted.

With the sun disappearing beyond the horizon, several servants were fluttering down the halls to light the torches and candle chandeliers above crossway points. There was a bit of a draft, and Hakim was grateful that he had packed his thick cloaks and trousers, for he knew that the weather could always be temperamental in the city. Besides, it was not like the estate back home. While it was large in size, and definitely reflected his royal status, it was minuscule compared to a castle. A few fires burning through the night would be enough to heat the bedchambers. Keeping the palace warm was a task all on its own.

Ivan walked at a brisk pace. It was not exactly difficult to match his stride, but Hakim did have to put more of an effort in so that he did not appear to be out of shape. After zigzagging through the main hallways, they finally arrived in front of a set of steel double doors.

Standing in front of them brought back a wave of memories; some good, some bad. There had been moments during the last war when the two brothers feared that the royal city would be infiltrated by King Castilian's army, but their troops were ultimately able to hold them off long enough for the truce to take place. If they had lacked the manpower during those cold, dark nights, Hakim wondered if Raimore would still be standing today.

Normally, when someone of his status entered a room, one of the guards would make an announcement to state his presence. That had not been the case for the war council room. Ivan fiddled with a gold key on his waist belt before unlocking the door and ushering Hakim inside.

He poked his head into the room, his eyes landing on the king, who had been standing at the round table in the center of the room. "Your Majesty, I will be stationed outside this door until the two of you are finished. I will not allow a single person inside until you give me the go-ahead."

"Thank you, Ivan" King Umar nodded. "We appreciate your loyalty and discretion."

With that, Ivan bowed to the brothers before shutting the doors firmly behind himself. There was an audible click as he locked the door from the outside. Hakim hovered in the shadows momentarily, collecting his thoughts.

"You're probably wondering why I've asked you here tonight," Umar murmured. There was a slight hesitation in his voice, as if he were afraid to say the reason out loud.

Hakim let out a deep sigh before joining his brother at the table. There were no seats around it, nor any in the room—only a map of their kingdom and the neighboring ones that surrounded it. Taviel was the one they shared borders with, and the one they had the most issues with over the past couple of generations. No one knew when it originated—it had to have been long before their grandfather's time—for even he had no recollection of what started it all.

"It has been a long time since the two of us stood in this room, fearing Raimore's fate if we were to make the wrong decision," Hakim replied. "I must admit, I didn't think we would be back here so soon."

"Nor I," Umar sighed. "I'm worried about Jawar. What if this is not such a good idea after all? What if King Castilian executes him and then declares war upon us? Without a legitimate heir, we can have no hope for House Al Naseem."

Hakim studied his brother intently. He was staring at the old piece of parchment, his brows furrowed together, as he ran his fingers across the border that divided the two kingdoms. It had been a little over a week since the two of them broke the news to Jawar that he was leaving the only place he had ever called home. They had ripped him by root and stem, and expected him to pack up a few of his belongings and travel across the country to live in his enemy's kingdom, under their roof of all places. Had it been Hakim and his eldest son, he did not know whether or not he could send him away like Umar was doing now. But that was the price to be paid for being the crowned king and prince. Sacrifices were all they knew.

"You act as if death would be your only fate if that were to happen," Hakim scoffed. "Besides, the chances of that happening are very slim. You have nothing to fear, brother. Jawar is a brave young man. He has accepted this, he told me so himself."

"He did?"

"Yes." Hakim joined his brother at the table and rested a gentle hand on his shoulder before giving it a tight squeeze. "We spoke about it earlier this afternoon. He told me he is honored to be Raimore's peace offering. That he wouldn't want it to be anyone else but himself."

Umar let his head drop as he sighed with relief. "That alleviates some of my anxiety. I feared it would take all five years before he ever forgave me for making him do this for us."

"Why do I feel like that's not the only reason you called me here tonight?" Hakim began. "This could have waited until morning. Tell me, Umar. What's going on?"

"I have received word from Taviel," Umar admitted. "I told only those involved, but I sent a few of my best undercover spies to get a feel for the kingdom. I had them act as tradespeople from other lands. They assured me they were very discreet."

"Umar!" Hakim gasped. "If King Castilian ever found out about this—"

"I know," Umar hissed. "But you don't need to worry about that. All four of them have returned, but it's not good, brother. You and I both know that, while some of the lowborn and common people believe that magic has long since rid itself from our lands, that it still hides in the cracks and crevices and that magic wielders conceal their abilities from the rest of the world, for fear of retribution."

"I'm well aware of this," Hakim said, rubbing his temples furiously. He was growing tired of his brother dragging out whatever secrets he came upon in Taviel. "What does that have to do with Jawar?"

"It's not just about my son, it's about all of us. Something is living in Taviel. A sorcerer, so I'm told. He doesn't even try to hide the fact that he has magic, which means he's dangerous."

"How so?"

"You don't think King Castilian would use him to his advantage should the two of us go to war? We barely had a chance going up against his mortal army, but if he has a powerful sorcerer in his midst, we may as well start digging our graves now, because that's where we are going to end up."

"I didn't realize you had so little faith in Raimore!" Hakim fired back. "You must learn to have faith, Umar, or else your people will start to see the fear in your eyes. I can see it now, but that's only because I'm your brother."

"What should we do about the sorcerer, then? Hope he doesn't get involved?" Umar bellowed.

"Calm yourself. Did any of your secret scouts actually speak with this man? Or are they going off what the townsfolk have said?"

"They said they never met him, but the tales were extensive. It has been months that he's been in Taviel. Surely King Castilian is aware of him squatting in his kingdom."

"Exactly, so there's your answer. This sorcerer is likely just someone who is in the midst of traveling and has set up camp for a little while. Perhaps he's just gathering enough supplies to continue on and just so happens to be there while your son is preparing his journey. It's just a coincidence, Umar, nothing more."

Umar stood up tall and crossed his arms over his chest. Hakim was hesitant to match his stance, only because he did not want to come across as intimidating, or the fact that he already knew about the sorcerer prior to their conversation. He would never admit to the king that he had done some digging of his own, just to make sure everything went according to plan. It was not just his brother's kingdom at stake, but their entire family. For generations, an Al Naseem son has sat on the throne, and Hakim would do almost anything to make sure that it stayed that way.

"So you believe this sorcerer will be long gone before the threat of war makes its way to our home?"

"Yes, and if it makes you feel any better, I will make sure that he does go. Whatever it takes. But you're getting all worked up over nothing, you see. Jawar leaves soon, and I have decided to join him on his journey there, as his personal escort. While he won't have anyone staying there, I thought it was the least I could do to ensure he gets there in one piece. It's my duty as his uncle to protect him as if he were my own flesh and blood."

"Thank you, brother," Umar said, placing a hand over his heart. "You have no idea how much this means to me."

"You should get some rest. It won't be long now before your son departs, and five years without him will feel like a lifetime."

"You're right, as usual. Remember, you cannot speak a word about this to anyone, not even Jawar. I don't need him stirring up trouble the second he steps foot in Taviel."

Chapter 3:

Welcome to Taviel

"That should be the last of it."

Jawar dusted his hands together as if he were the one who had done all the packing, but in reality, he had merely delegated all the tasks to his staff. It had been two weeks since his father revealed that he was going to be living in Taviel for the next five years. Jawar was not ashamed to admit that he had gone to his bedchambers that dreaded night and cried himself to sleep. He felt like he was not ready to leave home yet; he was only thirteen, and he had never been apart from his parents for more than a few days, if that. Now he was expected to spend five years in an entirely new country, living under their enemy's roof as if they were friends? It was an odd situation, but after some reflection with Usha, he came to realize that it was a blessing in disguise.

Not only was Jawar going to be able to help his kingdom, family, and home, but those of Taviel as well. He was going to learn all about their unique culture, their political views, history, and the lifestyle of those born high and low. What Jawar was most excited about was getting the opportunity to do something new. Not once had he ever gone beyond the borders of the royal city, and there was so much he was going to get to do and see—things he could have only dreamed about before.

"Three trunks, Your Grace? That's all?" Tierra, a middle-aged servant asked.

She raised an eyebrow in confusion, grabbing the last one from the bed and handing it to someone who was on their way out of the room. Others had already started placing sheets over all of the furniture to keep it protected until he returned. His bed had been stripped, leaving only the mattress and frame behind. His wardrobe and a small desk in the corner had been covered, as had the hand-carved chest at the foot of his bed. He did not have many possessions, nor did he wish to carry a heavy load to his new home. He had only packed the essentials—clothes for every season, a few trinkets for adventuring should he have the time, a couple of personal items he had been gifted over the years from his parents that held sentimental value, and some books to keep himself entertained. If there was anything else he required in Taviel, he was hopeful that King Castilian would be more than accommodating.

"What else do you think I'll need?" he asked.

It was not meant to come across as rude or ungrateful, but rather, he wondered if he had completely overlooked something without realizing it. He glanced at Usha, who had been lingering by the door, but he shrugged, unsure himself.

"Oh, nothing, it's just, normally those who travel across the country usually take more with them, that's all," she murmured.

"Prince Jawar will be well-tended at the palace," Usha offered. "Besides, King Umar has also mentioned something regarding financial burdens. He'll never have to go without."

She nodded and proceeded to shove her hands in her apron before taking them back out. Tierra repeated this process several times while circling about the room, as if unsure what she was supposed to do next.

"Well, if that's everything," she sniffled, "I guess this is goodbye, Your Grace."

"Oh, Tierra" Jawar pouted. He hugged the woman who had been taking care of him since he was an infant. "I'm going to miss you very much. When I get settled, I'll be sure to write you a letter—you, and Usha. You two have been like second parents to me all these years."

"Oh hush," Tierra blubbered. "We were just doing our jobs, is all."

"I'm grateful for it. I don't know what my life would have been without you in it."

"No doubt, you would have found yourself in a lot more trouble if we didn't pull some strings," Usha snickered, "or have you forgotten about that time you set all the chickens from the coop free and I had to go down and break the lock to look like it malfunctioned?" Jawar's face flushed with embarrassment, but they all laughed at the memory. "But, it's time to go now, little prince. Your uncle will be waiting in the carriage as we speak."

Tierra gave Jawar a sloppy kiss on his cheek before giving him a little push towards the door. His personal guard placed a hand over his shoulder as he escorted him out, and before he knew it, he was walking down the palace steps. His stomach was twisted in knots, knowing that it would be the last time he would do this for a while.

King Umar and Queen Jacia stood hand in hand outside the carriage. They wore matching garments similar to the one that Jawar had on, uniting them as a family, now and forever. He jumped into his mother's arms first, burying his face in the crook of her neck. She cried softly, squeezing him with all her might.

"I love you so much," she whispered. "You are the light of my life, and I'm so proud to call you my son." Releasing her death grip, she cupped both of his cheeks in her hands and kissed his forehead. "You behave yourself while you're in Taviel. Mind your manners, be polite, and learn as much as you can."

"I will," Jawar promised. His chin bobbed up and down, and tears pricked his eyes, but none fell. "I love you."

"Now you listen here, Jawar." His father grabbed Jawar by the chin and forced him to look at him. Something was glistening in his eyes, love of course, but underneath it was a flicker of darkness that Jawar could only describe as pain. "This is not an adventure I want you to take lightly. You have a duty to the crown and the kingdom to uphold the truce between our two nations. It all falls on you, and I know that might seem like a heavy burden to bear, but it's the price of—"

"Being a prince. I know, Father. I've been hearing that my whole life. I'm ready, I swear."

"That's my boy. We'll miss you here. I'm not sure what Usha is going to do when he is not chasing after you every day."

"I'm sure I'll find something to occupy my time while you're gone, little prince," Usha winked. "Here, I have something for you." He handed Jawar a leather-bound notebook with hundreds of empty pages. "Write down everything that happens, and when you return, I want you to read it to me. It'll feel as if I was there, right alongside you."

Jawar hugged his personal guard quickly before straightening himself out. "Thank you."

He opened the carriage door and slipped in on the opposite side of his uncle. Two others were following behind until they reached the royal city in Taviel.

"Are you ready, nephew?" Hakim asked, glancing up from the stack of papers in his lap. "It'll be a few days before we arrive, so you best settle in and enjoy the ride."

"Yes," he nodded, waving to his parents as the carriage pulled away toward the lower city. "I'm ready for anything."

***

The ride to Taviel proved to be more or less uneventful in Jawar's eyes, but he did not care that much.

He was distracted by a constant flow of thoughts about his adventure, and unable to think about things as menial as time going by, so it had felt like the blink of an eye. They had stopped every night to rest the horses, and the guards had been gracious enough to pitch Jawar and his uncle a canvas tent to sleep in. It had been a tad bit uncomfortable curling up on a thin piece of fabric, as opposed to his plush mattress back in the castle, but he made do. Hakim had said that he had seen far worse conditions while they were in the middle of a war. He used to sleep up against boulders a few hours at a time and that was it.

As for his uncle, he did not share more than a few words here and there during the entire course of the trip. He had been preoccupied with other things, so entertaining Jawar was not on his list of priorities. When Jawar had asked what was keeping him so busy, his uncle merely said that it was matters that did not concern him and that was that.

Jawar was tempted to peek at the papers that his uncle had been writing and reading all that time, but sadly, Hakim slept with them underneath his pillow, so he did not get the chance.

The only other thing that Jawar remembered from his travels were the guards at the border stopping them briefly. After flashing their documentation and the seal of King Umar, the Taviel guards sent them on their way without any further questioning. That was to be expected, since King Castilian was expecting Jawar's arrival.

Entering the new country was like going into a completely new world. The land was so much different than Raimore. They passed through lush forests so dense that he could only see a few trees deep before the view turned into complete darkness. They cut through a valley between two mountains, which Jawar was unsure about. It had become so narrow, that he feared that carriages would not be able to fit. Still, with a few scratches against the wood, they made it to the other side virtually unharmed.

Surprisingly, the royal city was fairly close to the Raimore border. In fact, it had only taken the troupe a few hours before they made it to the market district of the city.

Jawar stuck his head out of the window to drink it all in, even though his uncle clearly disapproved. He had attempted to lure his nephew back into the confines of their carriage with conversation, but Jawar was much too interested in the outside world to care. They had a vibrant marketplace back home, but this felt so new and lively, that his eyes never lingered in one place for more than a few seconds.

A bright flash of light burst in the streets, leaving a puff of smoke in its wake. The crowd surrounding the empty space applauded, and Jawar wished that he had seen what was so exciting.

"Uncle, I think they have magic here!" Jawar concluded. "I think a man just disappeared!"

"Don't be foolish," Hakim chastised. "Magic wielders are merely mythical—just a folktale that parents tell their children to keep their imaginations alive. But you're not a child, not anymore. You need to start acting like it, so sit down and stop hanging your head out of the window like a dog."

Jawar slumped back onto the bench seat and crossed his arms over his chest, glaring at his uncle. "What are you working on today?"

"We've been over this a hundred times," Hakim sighed. "It's business for your father and that's all I'm permitted to say."

"I'm the Prince of Raimore. Have you forgotten?" Jawar tilted his head to the side, hoping to taunt his uncle enough so that he would accidentally let something slip.

Hakim was well versed in children's antics though, having three children of his own. Grumbling under his breath, he rolled up a half dozen scrolls and stuffed them into the bag that he always kept on his person.

"That title won't matter anymore soon. Yes, you're a foreign prince, but to the Taviel people, you're also an enemy. It's unlikely you'll make friends here, so it would be best for you to keep your mouth shut and do as you're told. We're all relying on you to make this truce work. I would hate to have to return to your father in a few days and tell him that we're going to war all because you could not keep your opinions to yourself."

Jawar opened his mouth to snap back at his uncle for speaking to him in such a manner when the carriage came to a halt. He peered outside to find a massive castle looming over them in a cobblestone courtyard. Hakim stepped out first before offering Jawar a hand. Glancing upward, he was at a loss for words. It did not sit on a hill like the one back home. Instead, it was a mere few steps up off of the ground. The castle was a light gray in color and almost appeared as if it was all sculpted from the very same stone, which Jawar thought was impossible.

An older man with pale skin approached them, and since he was flanked by three guards on either side, Jawar assumed that he was King Castilian of Taviel. By his side was another man, his son perhaps, as they resembled each other down to the shape of their noses. His heart ached momentarily as he thought of his father, who was now several days' travel away from him.

"Welcome to Taviel," the older man said, opening his arms wide in greeting. He flashed a toothy smile, stepping forward to shake Jawar's hand. "You must be Prince Jawar. I have heard much about you from your father's letters. I must admit, I was expecting a little thing, not a young man such as yourself."

Jawar's eyes flickered to Hakim before he found the courage to speak. "And you must be King Castilian, I'm grateful that you have accepted my father's token of truce. I hope to learn a great deal about Taviel while I'm here."

"And learn you shall." King Castilian nodded. "This is my eldest son, Prince Darrow. I'm sure you two will grow to be friends. You'll be spending a lot of time together over the next couple of years. I expect you to keep up with your learning, as well as with some other duties around the kingdom."

"He's very intelligent," Hakim interjected. "Jawar is well versed in literature and politics. He shadowed his father nearly every day for the past year."

"Excellent," the king confirmed. He turned to Jawar's uncle, and while tilting his head slightly to the side, he inquired, "I apologize. King Umar never said who would be escorting the young prince across the border. You are?"

"Lord Hakim, I'm King Umar's brother and Prince Jawar's uncle."

"I see the family resemblance," Castilian acknowledged. "Well, since it is getting late in the afternoon, you and your troops are more than welcome to stay in the royal city overnight before heading back to Raimore."

"We appreciate the hospitality, Your Majesty," Hakim began, "but we really must resume our journey. It is a long way back to the royal city and we cannot afford to lose any time. My duty was to bring my nephew to Taviel safely, and that I have done."

"If that is what you wish," King Castilian replied. "I'm sure we'll be in touch with your brother soon enough."

"Farewell, Jawar. Remember all that we have taught you."

His uncle disappeared into the carriage without so much as a hug or any sort of display of affection. Jawar stood there, his face flushed, as he watched the last of his family ride off into the distance and out of sight. Surprisingly, King Castilian and Prince Darrow stayed by his side until the last of the Raimore carriages vanished out of sight.

"Can I ask you a question, Jawar?" King Castilian asked.

"Anything, Your Majesty."

"Are you afraid of me?"

"I don't know… should I be?"

"No," King Castilian smiled. "I think your time here will be good for both of our kingdoms. You'll see that we're not that different from those you know, and I hope that our bond will expand beyond our sworn obligations."

"Friends?" Jawar extended his hand out to his new guardian, who grasped it tightly with both hands.

"Yes, friends."

Chapter 4:

The Sword in the Stone

It was a prosperous afternoon in the Taviel marketplace for all but Merlin.

The place buzzed with citizens fluttering about the streets, cutting bargains with the merchants, and indulging in something lavish if their coin purses had a few extra pieces to spare. Sweet, delicious aromas wafted from the beloved bakery that always had crowds of people coming in and out of the doors. The baker was the best in the business, or so that was what Merlin had thought. His cakes were positively divine.

It was one of the perks of jumping nearly five centuries into the future; the food was better, the folks were friendlier, and the kingdom was a peaceful place to live. However, the only downfall was the fact that Excalibur had still not shown up. He had searched high and low for the mighty sword, overturned rocks, boulders, and snuck into people's houses while they were sleeping soundly, but still, it remained hidden from the world.

A part of him wondered if perhaps it was for the best that he had not found it. If he could not, the Djinn would never get his hands on it either.

"Master Merlin, please can you make it rain?"

A tiny set of hands tugged at the wizard's robes. He had been so distracted feeding off of the energy of those around him that he had not noticed the child at his side. The girl was not even tall enough to reach his knees. She stared at him with beautiful brown eyes that were full of hope and innocence. A woman who Merlin assumed was the girl's mother frantically shoved through the crowd, anxiously trying to close the gap between them.

"I'm not a master of anyone or anything," Merlin corrected. "I own no lands, nor do I have any titles that would allow me to become one. But I appreciate the compliment."

The child nodded, but he knew that she did not understand a single word coming from his mouth.

"Rain?" she asked once more, holding out a wilted bouquet of wildflowers.

"Ah, I see." Merlin scratched at his chin before dropping to a single knee so that he could speak to her at her level. He wished that he could remember what her name was to address her properly, but he had more important things to occupy his mind with. "I'm sorry, child, no amount of water will be able to bring those back from the dead. However, with a little bit of magic, they'll be as good as new."

With a lazy flick of his wrist, his eyes flashed a bright gold, and remnants of his magic glimmered in the sunlight. The flowers burst with light before standing upright in the girl's hands. She squealed like a newborn pig, drawing attention to the pair as people walked past. Merlin felt the judgment in their eyes, but he stood upright, not letting a single one of them see that it bothered him—which it did not. He was superior in every way possible. They just did not know any better.

"Sonya!" the child's mother gasped. She hoisted her child up onto her hip and hugged her tight. "What did I tell you about wandering off?"

"It's alright, Mama, I was safe with Merlin."

Sonya's mother glared daggers into Merlin's soul, her eyes narrowing as she shook her head slowly. "Have you no shame? It's one thing to parade around here showing what you can do, but to a child? She doesn't know any better."

"Magic is an extraordinary gift. You should be grateful she had the chance to witness it," Merlin retorted.

"It's evil and unnatural," the woman hissed. "You'd be wise to keep it under control before someone tries to steal it from you."

Grabbing the fresh flowers from her child's hands, she tossed them into the road, where they were immediately trampled by carriages and horses. The girl screeched, tears streaming down her face, but her mother did not flinch. She turned her nose up at Merlin and disappeared into the crowd without a single word.

You're not wrong, he thought to himself.

Some magic was indeed evil, or rather, the person who was wielding it could be. It was a weapon after all, and great and honorable kings could use it, or corrupt and vicious men. Merlin was neither. He was merely taught by the best sorcerer to have ever walked the earth.

Readjusting his robes, Merlin continued as if nothing had happened. He had a purpose—a routine more like it—and every afternoon, he stopped into the only blacksmith shop in town. It was run by a small family who were probably the only people in Taviel who could tolerate Merlin's quirks.

"You're late!" Neo exclaimed, as Merlin pushed through the swinging doors.

The blacksmith was stoking the fire before plunging an iron sword into it. As he did so, the sword glowed a bright red, and he quickly removed it before dipping it into a barrel of water. It sizzled instantly, and steam floated from the surface of the cold water.

"I was entertaining a child when its poor mother ruined all the fun," Merlin pouted.

Neo's daughter, Rosa, gestured toward the seat in the corner of the shop, just as she always did. At first, he had thought she was just being kind to him. He was not exactly old by any means, but he had figured that age had something to do with it. After a week or so, he had learned that she simply wanted him out of the way. It was easier to work around a rambling man who was seated than it was to dodge him while carrying hot coals as he paced up and down the shop.

"Let me guess. She did not appreciate your use of magic," Rosa wondered.

"Not in the slightest. What is it with you people and your distaste for the extraordinary?"

"The people of Taviel have long since forgotten magic in all its forms," Neo reminded him. "They fear what they don't understand. It's just that simple."

"I would teach them all about it if they gave me the chance," Merlin continued. "I wish everyone else were like you two."

"Sadly, that'll never happen," Rosa said.

Although she was barely old enough to be called a young woman, Rosa had been working for her father's business for some time now, or at least that was what she had told Merlin. He watched them silently as they worked, Rosa brandishing each of the weapons her father made with their signature seal. Neo was in charge of forging every blade, sword, and arrow for the king's army. If someone happened to admire his piece of handiwork and see the symbol, they would know where to go. Merlin thought it was absolutely brilliant.

"Might I ask if a sword not bearing your seal has come through since I was last here?"

Neo sighed and scratched the stubble of his beard before cleaning his hands on his filthy apron. "No magical sword has crossed this threshold."

Merlin's nose twitched, but he tried his best to appear unphased by this non-surprising revelation. He knew in his heart what the blacksmith's answer was going to be, but still, he had to ask.

"I still don't know why you think it would end up here," Rosa interjected.

Merlin and Neo both glanced at her with curious eyes. Realizing they were both waiting for an explanation, she cleared her throat before waving her hand nonchalantly. "Think about it—a beautiful sword falls into your lap out of thin air. You suspect it might be magic, and that means it's valuable, priceless even. Why go to the blacksmith shop? To get a second opinion? No, if Elixir is out there somewhere, it's probably hidden beneath someone's floorboards."

"Excalibur."

"Sorry?"

"The sword is called Excalibur."

"Does it really matter at this point?" Rosa raised an eyebrow before walking over to Merlin and placing a hand on his shoulder. "There comes a point when you have to stop searching for something that is lost forever."

"Things are only lost because they have not been found," Merlin stated. Standing from the rickety old stool, he patted Rosa on the head before tossing a coin to Neo. It was part of his routine—if he were going to annoy the father-daughter duo, the least he could do was to pay them for their time. "I'll see you both tomorrow."

Merlin was afraid to admit that he had reached a standstill regarding the finding of the sword. He still had hope, sure, but months and months without so much as a clue as to where it could have gone was not helpful. But he was not about to give up. So many great and honorable men sacrificed their lives to get Excalibur to him, just so that the Djinn could not abuse its power. He was not about to taint their valiant efforts by shrugging his shoulders and accepting defeat.

Stepping out of the scorching hot blacksmith shop, Merlin pulled the hood of his cloak over his head and slipped into the thick crowd. This had also become part of his routine before he headed home for the afternoon to his cottage in the woods—blend into the horde of people going about their daily business to search every man, woman, and child for any glimpse of Excalibur's hilt. Perhaps Rosa was on to something—if a commoner had indeed come across the mighty sword before Merlin did, why would they risk giving it up? A magical object such as that was beyond priceless and could alter a man's life in the blink of an eye.

He scanned his immediate surroundings with a careful eye until something shimmered at a man's hip. The pommel of his sword—could it be? Merlin squinted, trying to get a better look, concluding that it was indeed brandished with a yellow stone.

Merlin jumped in front of the man before he could even talk himself out of the situation. Reaching for the weapon, the man grabbed Merlin by the wrist and shoved him back.

"What do you think you're doing?" he shouted. "You must be the worst pickpocket in all of history!"

"Your sword—let me see it," Merlin heaved. "Now!"

Snarling his lip back in protest, the man obliged, but only tugged the blade a few inches out of its sheath. Merlin blinked several times, studying it before his cheeks flushed pink. What he thought had been the yellow stone of the legendary sword had turned out to be the innocent man's belt buckle.

"Satisfied?" the man questioned.

Frustrated and embarrassed, Merlin tugged on his fallen hood and shoved past the man. He had enough excitement for one afternoon. He would just start fresh in the morning, like he always did. A good night's sleep and a warm meal would cheer him up, or so he hoped. There was nothing else he could do about it now.

Leaving the marketplace took no time at all, and Merlin felt a rush of relief as he stepped onto the overgrown path. He could not say exactly why he chose an old, abandoned cottage to take refuge in. Perhaps it had something to do with his previous living arrangements. The tent had not been much back then, but it had been home. Besides, the forest was home to many creatures, some of which still held their magical abilities. It had been abundantly clear that only those with the power to wield magic could see them for what they truly were.

Merlin had been singing a song that he remembered from his time when a bright flash nearly blinded him. He halted instantly, rubbing his eyes with his closed fists. The hair on the back of his neck stood up, the magic within him sensing another's presence. He could only assume it was someone with immense power.

Stepping lightly, he ducked beneath a massive shrub, hoping that whoever or whatever it was had not seen him. He held his breath as he listened closely for any sign of movement. When only the gentle rustling of the leaves above him could be heard, he exhaled and opened his eyes. What he saw next made his heart practically drop into his stomach.

Just a few paces ahead, in a gigantic boulder concealed by the thick hedges that hid him, was the hilt of a magnificent sword. The sun shone through the yellow gemstone, making it appear as if it were made of gold.

Excalibur!

But how could it be? Merlin must have walked down this path more than one hundred times in the past few months, and never once had he come across the sword until now.

It did not matter. All he cared about was that he had found it. And now that he had, he was never going to let it go.

Chapter 5:

Merlin the Magnificent

"Run along now. Taviel is your home, you may as well get to know it a bit more," King Castilian prompted.

He had been gracious enough to allow Jawar a few days to settle into a routine before assigning him to certain responsibilities around the kingdom. That had also meant that he had been excused from his morning tutoring, which he did not mind, although he loved learning. With the afternoon to himself, Jawar did not know where to start. He had never been given such freedom, even in Raimore. There were always things to do, councils to sit in and listen to, and royals to meet and greet.

Jawar could hardly remember the last time he was permitted to go out and explore. Today he was not going to waste a single second of it. The sun was shining, the birds were singing, and there were many people in the courtyards. Jawar's cheeks ached from how much he had been smiling.

"Hello." He greeted a young couple as he walked past them. "Good afternoon," he said to an elderly man who was hobbling along next to his cart.

Guards acknowledged his presence with a quick bow of their heads. They had all been informed of his arrival, or at least that was what the king had said. As long as he wore King Castilian's seal on his collar, no one would disturb him.

On the way into the royal city the night before, Jawar had been intrigued by the dense forest just outside of the marketplace. The king had said that he could do whatever he wanted to, as long as he did not leave the city borders beyond the walls. Since those walls were beyond the dense woods, that meant that he was allowed to chase butterflies and climb trees in the forest to his heart's content.

While he was not entirely familiar with the layout of the marketplace, it was not difficult to spot the lush treetops in the distance, so he used them as his guide through the winding streets. Delicious scents tempted him a couple of times to make stops along the way, but he had forgotten his coin purse back in his bed chambers, and he did not hold the same status in Taviel as he did in Raimore. It was unlikely that any of the shop owners would feel so inclined as to give him free samples.

But Jawar did not care all that much about snacking on delicious treats. He would have his fill of them once he returned to the castle that evening. The forest called to him, like a whisper in the wind, and he was eager to find out why.

As he left the loud marketplace behind him, Jawar was a bit confused about the untamed path that laid before him. He could have sworn that the bush had been trimmed back far enough for the carriages to pass, but then again, he may have misjudged where they had come through. Looking back over his shoulder, he hesitated about going any further. He nibbled at the corners of his thumbnails, contemplating what he should do. It would be awfully embarrassing if he managed to get lost during the first few days of being in Taviel. Then again, he really did not want to give up and turn back.

Weighing his options, Jawar decided that he would not travel very deep into the forest. He was sure that, as long as he maintained sight of the castle, he would be safe.

Exhaling a breath from his pursed lips, Jawar trekked on with his head held high. While his heart was racing a mile a minute, his anxiety seemed to fade more the further he went. It was as if the forest had offered a blanket of protection, for not a single thought, worry, or fear entered his mind. Instead, he lost himself in the bliss and solitude of the stillness around him. It turned out to be only a temporary state of being, as the sound of a branch snapping ripped him from his euphoric state.

He froze in his tracks. Looking down at his belt, he cursed himself for not bringing a blade or dagger. What if it were a beast? Or a smuggler who would have no issue striking Jawar down?

Ducking behind the nearest tree, Jawar spotted movement just up ahead. He tilted his head, trying to make sense of what he was looking at. It was a man dressed in peculiar garments. He had never seen so many bright colors in his life. But that was not what had been so odd about the situation.

The man, who Jawar guessed was perhaps a few years younger than his father, was circling around a massive rock. In the center was the hilt of an enchanting-looking sword. Squinting, Jawar could make out a yellow stone in the pommel. What confused him was how the blade ended up embedded in the boulder to begin with.

Taking a step forward to get a better look, a bundle of twigs crunched beneath his boots, and he dropped to the ground immediately. The last thing he wanted was to have this possible lunatic to think that he had followed him out here. Holding his breath, he listened intently for any sudden movements. After counting to 30, Jawar dared to look at the strange man, only to find him climbing awkwardly on top of the huge rock.

He made an awkward gesture with his hands, which glowed brightly before he gripped the hilt tightly. Staring at the sky above him, the man pulled the sword out of the rock as if it were made of butter. Jawar could not believe what he was seeing! It had been one thing to come across a sword stuck in a stone, but to watch a man—one getting on in his years—to yank it free as if it were nothing. The only possible explanation was that he was dreaming.

The man jumped off of the rock and did a little dance, making Jawar giggle. He covered his mouth with the crook of his elbow so that the whimsical man would not hear him. Moments later, the man wrapped the blade in a piece of fabric from his sack and tucked it underneath his arm before running off down the makeshift path.

Disregarding all precautions, Jawar went to chase after the man, having many questions about what had just happened. But when he reached the path himself, he was confused to find no presence of the man at all—not even the sound of his footsteps.

It was as if he had disappeared into thin air.

***

Jawar stared at the empty path for what had felt like hours before he promptly headed back to the castle.

He could not say for certain what had transpired with the sword and the stone, but he knew that it was *not* nothing. Jawar had read tales when he was a child about the wonders of magic, and while his parents always said that they were merely legends and myths, nothing about that strange man made any logical sense. It would have taken at least 10 men to dislodge that sword. And even if he were strong enough to do it himself, where had the man gone? Surely Jawar would have heard him as he ran through the forest, but only silence had enveloped him.

None of it made sense. Worst of all, he did not get a good enough look of the man, so he would never be able to identify him should he cross paths with him again, unless he wore those colorful garments.

The second his boots hit the cobblestone road of the marketplace, Jawar grounded himself back into reality. As much as he wanted to know more, he knew that he could not very well bring this matter to King Castilian. He could not risk his new guardian thinking that he was too childish to be trusted with important duties. No, this was something he would have to keep to himself.

Turning down a random street, Jawar's eyes flickered to a young girl standing on the footpath, home of some of the busiest shops in the market. She had beautiful brown skin and hair concealed beneath a silk wrap. She discarded a bucket of water into the street before drying her hands on her apron.

Jawar looked up at a sign above the shop. It read "Neo's Smithy" in huge letters. Unable to stop himself, Jawar crossed the street without even looking and walked straight up to the girl.

"Hello." He smiled. "I hope you don't mind me saying, but that's a beautiful head wrap."

The young girl looked either appalled by his compliment or shocked, and Jawar could not pinpoint the exact expression. She touched the top of her head gingerly, having noticed the pin on his collar.

"You're a royal," she concluded. "But you don't look like King Castilian."

Jawar laughed at the obvious differences between their two families. "I'm his ward. I just moved to Taviel. I'll be staying here for a while."

He had never discussed with his father, or King Castilian for that matter, exactly who he was allowed to share the nature of their arrangement with. If the country believed that the two kingdoms were feuding to the point that they needed a token of truce to maintain order, he feared that both countries would fall into despair. It was best if he did not divulge any royal secrets to a commoner.

"Oh." She blinked. "Wait, you must be Prince Jawar of Raimore!" Realizing who was standing on her shop's stoop, the girl bunched up her dress and curtsied as best as she could. "I apologize, Your Grace. I didn't realize who I was speaking to. You must forgive my ignorance."

Jawar's face burned with embarrassment. He could feel the eyes of everyone on the path looking in their direction. The last thing he wanted was to draw any unnecessary attention to himself, and so with a gentle hand, he motioned towards the door, hoping that she would oblige without question.

"Sorry, would you like to come inside?" she offered, standing upright.

"If you wouldn't mind," Jawar said.

The two of them slipped inside and he closed the door quickly behind them, peeking out into the street to ensure that no crowds were headed their way. Sighing with relief that everyone had instead gone about their business, Jawar relaxed his shoulders and took a turn about the room.

"Rosa, darling, what's taking you so—" An older man stepped out of the swinging doors that led to the back half of the shop before he spotted Jawar standing awkwardly by the window. "Hello, young man, how can we help you?"

"This is Prince Jawar, Papa." Rosa beamed. "All the way from Raimore."

"Your Grace." Her father bowed. "It's an honor to have you here. Please, call me Neo."

The blacksmith and his daughter both fiddled with their hands, as if they were unsure how they were supposed to act in the presence of royalty. Jawar assumed that they did not have much experience with King Castilian and his family, despite their shop being so close to the castle.

"While I might be a prince where I'm from, here I'm just Jawar. Don't let me interrupt if you have work to do, I was just passing by and felt compelled to talk. I don't know many people here and your daughter...

Well, she looks about my age, so I thought it would be nice to have a friend."

"A prince and the blacksmith's daughter as friends?" Rosa smirked. "I'm not sure King Castilian would approve."

"Oh," Jawar grunted. "Well, I should be on my way then. I've just come from a walk in the forest. They are probably expecting me back at the palace."

"You have come from the forest?" Neo asked. "I don't mean to offend you, but have you no blade on your person, Your Grace?"

"No," Jawar began. "I have some of course, just not on me. I didn't think about it when I left, to be honest."

"Taviel is a peaceful kingdom, as I'm sure you know, but someone of your status should never be without a blade. Here—" Neo slipped through the swinging doors momentarily before returning with a simple dagger. "A gift. We supply the royal army with all of their weapons. I assure you it is well made."

Jawar took the dagger and admired its fine quality. He had seen many blades in his life, but none quite as exquisite as this one. He held it to his heart and nodded his head. "Thank you, Neo. That's very kind. Are you the only blacksmith around here?"

"That's right," Neo confirmed. "Why, is there something you're looking for?"

"No." Jawar shook his head. He was not entirely sure how to phrase his next question. "It's just that I saw a magnificent sword earlier, along with a very odd man. I was curious to know if it was your handiwork or not."

"An odd man?" Rosa interjected. "He wouldn't happen to be wearing a unique set of robes?"

"Yes!" Jawar exclaimed. "Do you know him?"

Neo and Rosa exchanged a look before the blacksmith nodded. "Indeed, we know him. He's fairly new to the city, just like you. His name is Merlin. He's got a bit of a reputation. Some claim he's a sorcerer, but that's just talk. Still, it may be best if you steer clear of him, for your own sake."

"Alright, if you say so," Jawar agreed. "And the sword?"

"He has come in every day for the past few months looking for it," Rosa explained. "By the sounds of it, he has finally found it. I'm happy for him. He was going right mad trying to find it."

Neo nodded, and Jawar sensed that, while the two were happy to entertain the little prince, they had work to do that required their attention. The last thing he wanted was to be a burden to them.

"Well, I should get going. Thank you, Neo, for the gift. It is lovely. Rosa, I hope to see you again soon."

"If you need me, you know where to find me."

Chapter 6:

The Curse of Excalibur

Jawar's first week with the tutor had been both exhilarating and exhausting.

He was grateful that Prince Darrow was also learning all the same material that he was. Of course, he had grown up in Taviel, so his knowledge of the kingdom was far superior to Jawar's. He could name every last city by heart, identify the types of plants and animals native to their country, recite when they had gone to war, and how many casualties they had on record—you name it. Jawar always felt slightly uncomfortable when they were learning about the history aspect, as a lot of it overlapped with Raimore, and not always in a good way. Luckily, their Master Tal did not hold any judgment over Jawar's lineage.

"It's a part of any country's history," he had said, when Jawar asked if they could skip that lesson. "It's important for you to know what has happened, so the two of you can make sure it does not happen again."

Prince Darrow had given him an encouraging squeeze on the shoulder, assuring that they were not enemies. Years down the road, the two of them would be the kings of Taviel and Raimore, and they would be at peace.

All the other subjects had been a breeze. Outside of history, politics, and geography, they were soon going to learn about the economics of the whole country. In fact, it had been one of the things that King Castilian had wanted Jawar and Darrow to learn about the most, as he had planned a project for them in the coming years. While Taviel was a harmonious land, like most kingdoms, many people suffered from poverty, and he wanted to help as much as he could—Even if that meant re-evaluating the taxes and cutting costs on the royal families and estate holders.

It was as if he had stepped into an entirely new world. His Uncle Hakim never talked about those sorts of things, even though he helped Jawar's father to manage the kingdom's finances. Jawar wondered if he would be stepping out of place if he brought it up the next time that he saw his relatives.

After each lesson, Master Tal allowed Jawar to linger in the library so that he could catch up on some reading, as Prince Darrow had already done most of the work before his arrival.

Today was another one of those days, and as soon as the double doors were latched shut, he began walking down the rows of bookshelves, one by one. Master Tal had organized all the books in alphabetical order, so Jawar could easily find a book about whatever he wanted to learn after the lesson. He thought it might be a good idea to brush up on the different social statuses of Taviel. While he figured that they were most likely similar to those of Raimore, it would not hurt to check.

Locating the *S* section of the library, he ran his fingers across the spines of the books until he stopped suddenly, his eye catching a curious title.

Sorcery: The Complete Guide of Sorcery in Taviel.

Jawar's heart pounded in his chest. He glanced down both sides of the aisle, feeling as if someone might be watching him. When he determined he was, in fact, alone in the library, he slipped the book off of the shelf and held it with both hands. It was covered with a thick layer of dust, as it had likely been untouched for years, decades even.

He had wanted to ask Master Tal about sorcerers after what Neo had said about the mysterious Merlin. However, the warning was what had held him back. The fact that he had mentioned that he had a reputation, and one that was not necessarily the best, made him hesitate. The last thing he wanted was to go stirring up trouble during the first few weeks that he had been in the kingdom.

But now that he had the book in his hands, the temptation to know was too much to resist.

Scurrying over to the table he had been working at, he brushed the cover of the book with his sleeve, removing some of the dust. He carefully opened the book to the first few pages, making sure to take extra care, as there was no telling how old or fragile the book was. While the pages were yellowed and the text had faded, it was still legible. What surprised him most was the fact that some of the drawings were colored, which was rare for a text as old as this. He had seen few books during his studies that had such incredible detail, and hoped that it attributed to the legitimacy of its contents.

"Names of registered sorcerers in Taviel, magical creatures, list of spells, and ancient artifacts," he read out loud, stopping at the last one.

Something gnawed in the pit of his stomach. It was similar to the feeling he got when he had first walked into the forest that afternoon. It was as if he was fated to witness Merlin retrieving the sword, and also to stumble upon this book about sorcery. Was it all coincidence, or was the universe pointing him down another path? Jawar liked to think of himself as a logical, rational person, but leaving Raimore and stepping into a new world had opened his eyes to new possibilities. Maybe, just maybe, that included magic.

Scrunching up his nose, Jawar flipped through the hundreds of pages until he found the last section of the book. Surprisingly, it was the biggest of all of the parts of the book. Apparently, there were plenty of ancient artifacts in Taviel. This part of the book also had a glossary section, but none of the names sounded familiar, or mentioned a sword. He would just have to go page by page to see if anything stood out.

Starting with the letter *A*, there were amulets, belts, crystal balls, even enchanted dice that could show someone their fate. Flipping to the next page, he brought the book up to his face so that he could focus on one of the drawings better. It was a sword, and in the pommel, there was a bright yellow stone.

"The Curse of Excalibur," he read aloud, running his finger across the script at the top of the page.

This has to be it—the sword that Merlin had pulled from the stone. Although he did not get a close enough look of it at the time, there was no mistaking that hilt. It was the exact same, down to the shape of it.

He read on: *The Curse of Excalibur is one of the oldest legends in Taviel's history. Dating back to the very existence of magic, few who have been blessed to see the sword in person have lived to tell the tale. The origin of the sword remains unknown, and it has been centuries since it was last seen. Many believe that it never existed in the first place, but others claim that it was discarded in the Black Sea, along with several other dangerous relics. Despite the contradicting legends, Excalibur is one of the most powerful magical items to have ever existed—its abilities are said to bend the very laws of nature, but no one has had the chance to wield such power. Excalibur and its magic have been protected by a curse that shall condemn to death any person who touches.*

Jawar repeated the text in his mind: *A curse that shall condemn to death any person who touches it.*

But Merlin touched it. How can that be? Jawar witnessed it with his very eyes. Perhaps the person who had documented the relics got it wrong about Excalibur. Maybe there was a certain way that it had to be held for the curse to take effect.

Reading the last sentence at least a dozen times more, Jawar let out a frustrated huff and slammed the book shut. He felt like such a fool. There was no way that this sword was the one he had seen in the forest. Merlin had probably tricked him into thinking it was something important. A sorcerer like that surely would have heard Jawar stomping through the woods. He was just toying with him. It was all just a silly game and he had fallen for it.

Pursing his lips, Jawar pushed up from the table and put the book back where he found it. There was no point reading any further, for he had no interest in the sword anymore. Besides, it was careless for him to let his priorities stray from the real reason he had come to Taviel in the first place. It was not a time to escape from his duties as a prince. The fate of the neighboring kingdoms rested on his shoulders, and he would not let some wild man who lived in the forest ruin their futures.

Extinguishing every last candle in the library, Jawar headed for his bedchambers. It was getting late, and while his stomach growled from having eaten supper early, he was too tired to venture all the way down to the kitchen for a bite to eat. He would just have to hold off until breakfast.

Luckily for him, his sleeping quarters were in the same wing of the castle as the library. Not only did that mean less walking for him, but it also limited the likelihood of him getting lost. He had only been living in the castle for a few days, and it had a completely different layout than the one back home. Prince Darrow's rooms were not far from Jawar's, which he secretly appreciated. Since he had no siblings, it was nice to spend time with someone his own age.

He was nearly to his bedchamber when the sound of a man's voice startled him. "How is Prince Jawar getting along in his lessons?"

Jawar peered around the corner to find King Castilian and Prince Darrow walking straight toward him.

"Things are going well. Master Tal is exceptionally proud of how well he is advancing in such a short amount of time. It didn't come as a shock as he is a prince. He said that education is very important in Raimore."

"As it is here in Taviel," King Castilian confirmed. "And outside of the lessons? Are you two getting along?"

"Yes." Prince Darrow nodded. "He's perfectly pleasant. I wouldn't say we're the best of friends, but I see no reason to not like him."

"There's something I have to tell you, but it must remain between us." King Castilian lowered his voice and glanced down the hallway just as Jawar ducked out of sight. "I've received word from Raimore that King Umar has started preparing for war just in case things don't work out between our two families."

"Has there been a declaration made?"

"No," the king assured his son. "But he has started assembling his army, and I am told that they have been training new recruits and promoting some of the veteran soldiers to general status. Strictly speaking, they are all defensive maneuvers, but we must be vigilant."

"What will you have me do?" Prince Darrow asked.

"See what Jawar knows about his father's plans, but don't make it too obvious. I don't want to spook him and have him writing to King Umar about an attack. We do not want to go to war, do you understand? We are trying to prevent it."

"I understand, Father. I don't think Jawar wants to see his kingdom fall either. During the history lesson, he looked ashamed when we talked about all the casualties for both sides. He doesn't seem like the kind of boy who has a lust for blood and vengeance."

"He might not seem like it on the outside, but you would be surprised when given the choice. I have seen many great men fall to the temptations brought on by war. I know this is a bit of a burden I'm placing on your shoulders, but it's for the good of us all."

"I can handle it."

"Alright. Now, get some rest. We have a council meeting in the morning that I want you and Jawar to attend."

"Goodnight, Father."

The sound of advancing footsteps caused Jawar to scramble for a hiding place. Whipping open the closest door, he dove inside and shut it quietly, pressing his forehead against the wood. He counted to 50, giving King Castilian plenty of time to head up the stairs to where the king and queen's private bedchambers were.

Cracking the door open just enough to see through, he determined that the coast was clear before quickly exiting the unoccupied room and heading around the corner. To his luck, Prince Darrow had already retired into his bedchambers, making it a quick race down the hall and into his own. Once safely inside, he flopped down onto his bed and stared at the ceiling.

Why was his father resurrecting the army? None of it made any sense. He had been the one to suggest that Jawar become the token of truce for the two countries. Why would he declare war against a kingdom where his one and only heir currently resided? It had to be a mistake—Jawar's life depended on it.

Chapter 7:

The Force of the Djinn

Merlin's rickety old cottage was bursting with life and magic as he went about his usual business.

It was one of the perks of being taught by the most powerful sorcerer in the world. Though it had been years, and now perhaps centuries, since he had last seen his beloved tutor, he would never forget the old man. He had taught Merlin that magic is to be treated with love and respect, that it is a gift that should not be abused. He tried his best to live by these teachings, although he did bend the rules every now and again, just like he had with that child in the marketplace. Had it been a bit obnoxious to parade around the market showing his superior abilities for every mortal to see? Yes, but it had also brought wonder and joy to the little girl's life, and so it had been well worth the deviation.

Sitting cross-legged on the rotting floor, Merlin suspended a delicate amulet in mid-air. Magic glittered all around it, defying the laws of gravity to hold it up. With a gentle wave of his fingers, the amulet slowly turned so that he could examine it from all sides. It was a beautiful teardrop shape and had several amethyst chunks set around the main crystal. The chain was a solid piece of gold with a tiny clasp which held it together.

When Merlin had transported to this new land, he had not only been searching for Excalibur, but for magical relics too. He did this for two reasons. The first, and probably the most important, was to ensure that the powerful artifacts did not fall into the wrong hands. The Djinn had proven just how magic and power could corrupt a person. Merlin had made it his life's mission to protect magic from the destructive nature of humanity, even if that meant he would be isolated for the rest of his days. It did not matter. His life and soul were dedicated to following in the footsteps of his tutor.

The second, and a little bit more selfish reason, was to study the magical properties of the relics so that he could better understand them. The scriptures and ancient texts that were written about these ancient artifacts were not nearly as useful as one might think. He had scoured the castle's library during the first few weeks of arriving in Taviel and only managed to find a single book about sorcery. Sure, its pages were filled with real objects, creatures, and spells, but they had only scratched the surface on their information about them. Besides, most of the findings were written long after the artifacts had been seen, meaning, they had all but become legends by then—fiction even, as some would say.

The amulet hovering in the middle of Merlin's cottage proved otherwise. Scribbling in his notebook of ancient artifacts, he used a piece of charcoal to draw a realistic picture of the amulet, down to the very shape of the crystals. He wished that he had some dyes so he could capture the essence of the colors, but he would just have to do that at another time.

Reaching out, he released the magic with a quick snap of his fingers. It receded back into his body, giving Merlin a burst of energy. He was just about to test the abilities of the amulet, when the hairs on his arms stood up.

His head snapped toward the door, and he closed his eyes so he could tune into his other senses. A series of footsteps was quickly nearing the cottage. Merlin could not make out an exact number, but he guessed that there had to be between three and five people advancing. They were running at full speed and that was all Merlin needed to know.

They were coming for him!

Standing up, he grabbed a small leather pouch from his desk and slipped the amulet inside. Underneath the rug by his bed, he removed the floorboard, placing the relic with all of the other magical items he had collected.

He figured that they were a group of bandits who had caught wind of a sorcerer living within the bounds of the royal city and that he would be an easy target to steal from because he was old and alone. The cottage was located far beyond yelling distance, so no guards would hear his cries for help.

Merlin smirked a little bit as he walked out to the small porch of his cottage, patiently waiting for their arrival. It had been so long since he had a little fun with weak humans who did not know a thing about magic. It would be good practice, as he had felt like he had become a little rusty since traveling to Taviel.

One thing was for certain, they were not taking a stealthy approach to the cottage. The whole forest could probably hear them coming. The little critters would be taking cover in the undergrove or hiding in the hollowed-out tree trunks.

Scanning the area around his home, he spotted four men heading south. So, his suspicions appeared to be spot on. They were coming from the marketplace. What he did not understand was if they had heard about Merlin, surely, they must have also learned that he was a sorcerer. Who would knowingly go up against someone with magic? Especially in this new world, when many of the people thought that it was either fictitious or phased out from the country?

They ran down the path in a single formation, and as soon as they reached the clearing that Merlin had cleaned out when he first moved in, they all stood an arm's length apart, staring at Merlin without saying a word. He looked at them all individually, and his magic tingled beneath his skin. Something about this ambush was not right.

"Hello, young men," he called out, waving dramatically as if they were old friends. "What an unexpected surprise!"

The awkward silence was deafening. After a few beats, one of the bandits stepped out of line and held up his right hand. "Give us Excalibur and we'll let you live."

Merlin could not contain his laughter. He hunched over, placing both hands on his knees as he cackled like a court jester. The invaders did not seem the least bit phased by his actions. Perplexed, Merlin descended the three steps from his porch so that he stood on the same level as they did.

"How do you know about the sword?" he asked.

The man who had made the ridiculous request—their leader, Merlin assumed—tilted his head to the side. His eyes were a most unusual color. They were brown, but there was something different about them. They had a white haze, cloudy almost. He wondered if the men had been poisoned by something and were now delusional.

"Did you think you could hide from him?"

"Him, who?"

"The Djinn," the four said in unison. "No amount of space or time will ever be enough. You'll never outrun him."

Merlin's heart nearly stopped right then and there. It was not possible. It could not be. He left the Djinn behind when he traveled centuries into the future. He was the only one with a time-traveling artifact. At least, that was what he had been counting on when he fled. He was sure that his enemies would not be able to follow him.

"Is he here?" Merlin questioned.

His eyes focused beyond the four men standing in front of him, scanning the trees in the distance. If the Djinn was controlling these men, there was a good chance he was in this realm. And sadly, Merlin was wildly unprepared for another battle against the wicked sorcerer.

"Not in his physical form," one of the men replied. "But his mind and his sight are. He can see you, the sweat on your brow, and the fear in your eyes. You did not expect he would be able to reach you this far."

"You must be mistaken," Merlin growled. He lifted his chin and locked his jaw in place, standing his ground. "I fear no one."

"Give us Excalibur," they said together again, "and he'll spare your life."

"I'd rather die than hand it over. Besides, what makes you think I have it? We were separated when I landed in this kingdom. I have been searching for it ever since."

"Lies!" they hissed. "You initiated the prophecy when you removed the sword from the stone. It has begun. Hand it over, or you'll pay with your life."

The last thing Merlin wanted was to give them any sort of advantage. He had no idea what prophecy the Djinn was referring to, and he was not about to ask. Sadly, he made the mistake of looking over his shoulder. Before he had the chance to cast a protection spell on the cottage, the four men leaped into action.

The closest perpetrator tackled Merlin to the ground. Two others jumped up the three steps and burst through the cottage door, while the fourth helped to pin Merlin's hands down.

Fools. They thought if they disarmed his hands, he would become useless. Perhaps that would be true if he were a beginner magic wielder, one who had no control over his powers. But Merlin was no amateur. The magic coursed through his veins. It was a part of him, just like the air in his lungs and the bones in his body. They worked in harmony, as his magic and his soul had merged into one.

Squeezing his eyes shut, the two men struggling to keep him went flying through the air. They did not scream, or make any noise for that matter, as they were still under the careful control of his enemy. Merlin did not care to check if they survived the impact of smashing against a one-hundred-year-old tree.

Scrambling up the cottage steps, he ran inside to find that the two others had managed to locate Excalibur. The rug was bunched up, and the floorboards were torn apart, exposing all the magical items he possessed—the sword included.

The blade was still wrapped in the protective silk, with only the hilt uncovered. Lying in a disheveled mess were the two innocent souls who paid the price of touching the cursed blade.

Their hands were black, resembling pieces of charcoal after a night of burning in a fire. Merlin bet that if he made any attempt to move them, their hands would crumble to ash and blow away with the wind. Their eyes remained open, and unlike before, they had fear in them, for in their final seconds of life, the connection with the Djinn had been broken.

Letting out a painful sigh, he had almost forgotten about the other two before they came crashing inside.

"No, wait!" Merlin pleaded, placing himself between them and Excalibur. "It's not worth your life."

"Give us the sword," the leader said. "Now!"

Merlin turned to grab hold of Excalibur to keep them as far away from it as possible, but they attacked him from behind. The second man had just barely grazed his fingers across the hilt when he instantly fell to his knees. The darkness crept from the tip of his nail to where his wrist met his hand. He gasped, reaching for his throat as if the life were being choked from him.

The leader pounced on Merlin's back, stretching his arm out as far as he could to try to grab hold of the sword. Merlin could not find the strength to end the man's life before he cursed himself. In the past, he had done what was necessary to protect magic at all costs, and was ashamed to admit that he had spilled blood in the process.

But this was different. This man was innocent. His mind was an empty vessel that the Djinn had seeped into. Merlin could not begin to imagine that this young man had his whole life ahead of him. It was too painful to think about.

Before he knew it, the leader touched it and immediately slipped off of Merlin's back. Just like all the others, his hand turned to ash, and the life faded from his eyes in mere seconds.

At least the curse was merciful in that sense. It was a quick death.

Merlin stood in the center of all the dead bodies for a few minutes, saying prayers for each one of them in the hopes that they would find peace in the afterlife. None of this had been their fault—he knew that—and he would give them a proper burial. It was the least he could do.

First, he needed to conceal the sword, and this time, he would do it with magic. This had been his first encounter with the Djinn, but he knew it would not be his last. Wrapping it in the ancient silk, he placed the sword underneath the floorboards and covered it back up. Placing both hands on the rug, he cast a spell under his breath, one that would keep it hidden from everyone but him. They could rip the cottage apart, board by board, and still, no one would ever be able to find it.

Merlin could not handle the burden of another death. He knew deep down that it had been inevitable, but worst of all, that these four men were just the beginning of a long and gruesome battle against the wicked sorcerer.

This had just been a painful reminder that no matter how much time and distance he put between them, Merlin could not outrun his fate or destiny.

Chapter 8:

Curse of Curiosity

Jawar was embarrassed to admit how much Merlin's deceitful tricks had bothered him.

However, what infuriated him more was the fact that he was second-guessing himself, again. What if Merlin was just trying to make him think it was a game so he could keep the powerful sword all to himself? From the little that Neo had said about the man, Jawar would not put it past him. He seemed like the selfish type.

The thought that had continued to bounce around Jawar's head for the past two days was what Excalibur could do for Raimore and Taviel. The book on sorcery had limited information regarding its powers and abilities, but surely something like that might be exactly what they needed to establish peace, once and for all. As the token of truce, Jawar felt like it was his obligation to do whatever he could to ensure that war did not break out between the two kingdoms. The last thing he wanted was to disappoint his father because he had not been brave enough to face an eccentric old man.

In the limited free time he had been given since hearing the appalling revelation that his father was gathering an army, Jawar had come up with a makeshift plan. He had gone to the marketplace in the afternoon, telling King Castilian that he was eager to try some of the kingdom's delicacies. His guardian had told him to take his time, and even gave him the names of some of his favorite spots to visit. Everything seemed fine between the two of them on the surface, but Jawar could not forget what he had heard the previous night. King Castilian and Prince Darrow were keeping a close eye on Jawar to gauge just how much he knew about his father's plans.

While he had made a few purchases to maintain his rouse, Jawar had also asked a few of the shop owners about the sorcerer who lived in the woods.

"Oh, you must mean Merlin," the wonderful lady who worked in the bakery had said. "He's a bit strange, I will admit, but he's harmless. I think he's lonely. He comes into town almost every afternoon before trekking back out to the abandoned cottage."

"Yes, I know Merlin," a middle-aged man confirmed. He was a merchant who sold parchment, journals, charcoal, and ink. "Everyone in the city does. He hasn't been here for long, but he has certainly made a lasting impression. He's odd, but he means well, or at least I think so."

Everyone else that Jawar had spoken to said the same thing. Merlin was an unusual fellow who found more comfort living among the creatures and the unruly forest than in town with the rest of the folks. But despite his behavior and antics, he was kind, generous, and had even helped a lot of the people out when they needed it. He had brewed a special ailment that alleviated a man's back pain so that he could continue to work without having to give up everything he owned. He slipped coins into children's pockets when they were not looking, and even saved a young family from a group of vicious bandits who had tried to kidnap their son.

It made Jawar's head hurt trying to make sense of it all. Why had Neo warned him about going near Merlin if he was a hero in the people's eyes? Should he trust one man's opinion above everyone else's?

He felt no more prepared now than he did two days ago, when he first decided that he was going to steal the sword. But time was of the essence. The sooner he had it in his possession, the better he would feel.

Tonight was the perfect night to sneak out. King Castilian was called away for three nights on some business, although he had neglected to say what it was about. Prince Darrow had already retired for the evening, and the young prince and the queen were likely fast asleep in their beds on the floor above him.

Jawar's plan was simple. He was going to go down to the kitchens, and should he run into someone important, he would tell them that his stomach ached and needed a warm glass of milk. There was a servant's entrance in the kitchen, and he prayed it was unlocked, so that he could use it to venture down to the lower tunnels and make his way to the gates that he had found in the marketplace.

Packing a light sack of belongings, he put the strap over his head and buttoned his jacket over top of it so that no one would see. He could not very well look like he was going somewhere, or surely one of the guards would question him. He extinguished the oil lamp on the table beside his bed and the room fell into darkness. Stumbling his way to the door, he sucked in a deep breath and went on his way.

The kitchens were easy to locate. Not only had he been there many times, but the aroma from dinner still lingered in the hall outside. Creaking the door open, he took a quick glance around and found it to be empty. Slipping inside, he had just raised his hand to the servant's entrance door when a young woman walked through.

She gasped and her hand flew to her chest as she braced herself against the doorframe. "Your Grace! What are you doing out of bed at this time of night?" she asked.

"I apologize. I didn't mean to frighten you," Jawar stammered. "I had just come down for a glass of milk."

"Oh." She blinked. "Not feeling well?"

"No. I think I might have eaten too much at dinner. I'm fine though, you can go back to what you were doing."

"I can have one of the guards escort you back to your room if you wish," she offered, wanting to be helpful to the young prince. If she only knew that she was being the complete opposite.

"No, that's alright. I know my way back."

"Alright," she said hesitantly. "Goodnight, Your Grace."

She curtsied before sidestepping past him and disappeared out of the doors that he had initially come in. He did not realize that the servants worked so late in the night. He silently cursed himself and vowed that he would pay more attention to the staff's routines, just in case he needed to go out on another night's adventure in the future.

In the meantime, he waited a few seconds before going out of the doorway that she had come in through. It was dimly lit, and he wished that he had brought a lantern of some kind, but figured it was best that he had not. A light would only draw more attention, and he needed to become one with the shadows.

Walking down the eerie halls, he found a set of stairs that he prayed led to the gates that he had seen earlier that afternoon. He crept down them, making sure to make as little noise as possible. When he reached the bottom, he was pleased to recognize the buildings in the courtyard. However, he had not planned that they would lock the gates at night.

Shaking them vigorously, he clenched his jaw tight, fearing that he had gone all this way for nothing. Furious, he kicked at the gate with his boot, and one of them became dislodged from the hole in the ground, opening slightly. He realized that it was only locked by a chain, and if he pushed one of them far enough, he just might be the right size to squeeze through.

"Worth a try," he whispered to himself.

Pushing the gate with all of his might, he only gained a few inches, but it was adequate. Wedging himself between the two bars, he sucked in a deep breath and fell through onto the other side. His hands broke his fall, but they paid the price of getting stabbed by dozens of little rocks. It stung, but he swallowed the pain and pushed on, not wanting to be anywhere near the gates in case one of the guards had heard something.

He lingered strategically in the shadows on the walking paths in the marketplace, out of the light from the lanterns. The streets were empty, save for a few stray dogs that came up to him in search of food. His heart ached, wishing that he had grabbed something, even if it were stale bread from the kitchens, on his way out. Sadly, he had nothing to offer, so he continued toward the edge of the forest.

It had been difficult to locate the overgrown path in the dark, but after walking up and down for half an hour, he finally spotted it, thanks to the moonlight. He took a few steps, disappearing into the darkness, and then stopped. His heart was beating dangerously fast, and his palms were sweating profusely, despite his constant rubbing of them on his trousers. He had no idea why he was so afraid of coming face to face with the sorcerer. Perhaps it was because he had never met one before and did not know what he was capable of.

Deep down, he knew it was because of the sword. What if what he read in the book was true? What if he died the second that he touched it? He had brought gloves, just in case, but would that be enough?

Swallowing a lump in his throat, he trekked on, hoping that he would find some fraction of courage when he happened upon the little cottage.

After walking for over an hour, and nearly wetting himself when a little rodent ran across his boots, Jawar had spotted the cottage in the distance. The orange light glowing from the windows acted as a beacon, and when he crept up to the open clearing, he hovered at the tree line, calculating his next move. His plan had just been to sneak in and steal the sword, but he doubted that the sorcerer was asleep with all those candles lit. He would have to change tactics to get inside.

Stepping out from the cover of the woods, Jawar walked up the porch steps and knocked at the front door. He listened intently, and there was no sudden movement from inside. He knocked again, a little louder this time, wondering if perhaps Merlin was hard of hearing. Again, there was nothing from inside the cottage. Groaning, Jawar stepped in front of the closest window and peered inside. The cottage had but a single room and upon quick inspection, he realized that no one was home.

"Makes my life easier," Jawar concluded.

He opened the front door and was surprised by how much paraphernalia could fit into such a small space. Nearly every available surface was covered in the sorcerer's personal belongings. Dozens of books, loose pieces of parchment, and a few clothes were bunched up on the floor by the bed.

He started from one end of the room to try to locate the sword. Searching high and low, he discovered that it was not in the chest of drawers at the end of the bed, nor in any of the cupboards in the makeshift kitchen. He knew it had to be here somewhere.

As he moved to sit on the edge of the mattress, the floor creaked under his feet, and he froze in place. Looking down at the hideous rug, he shifted his weight from foot to foot and the floor creaked again.

"Well, well, well," Jawar snickered, dropping to his knees and throwing the rug out of the way.

A board was loose, and after wedging his finger on one side, it slipped out of place with ease. He gasped at the sight of so many trinkets. Most of them he could not identify, but a shiver went down his spine just the same, and he sensed that they were magical indeed. Resting on top, was a long piece of fabric. His hand hovered over top of it, but remembering what the book said, he fumbled for the gloves in his belt.

Once they were on, he gently lifted the entire piece of fabric and scooted over to the bed, laying it on the mattress. Holding his breath, he unfolded the first piece of fabric, and then the second, revealing the most exquisite piece of weaponry he had seen in his entire life.

Up close, it looked exactly like the one he had seen in the book—right down to the carvings on the blade. Squinting, he realized that it looked like a script of some kind, but it was written in a language he did not recognize. Based on how old this sword was, he figured that it was from a different time.

A branch snapped outside and Jawar looked at the door, forgetting that he had left it open. Merlin must have come back. He had to be quick.

The second he grabbed the hilt of the sword, the sorcerer burst into the room, his face drained of all life. "No!" he shouted, his arm extending out to stop Jawar, but it was too late.

Excalibur sent out a shockwave, knocking Merlin onto his rear end. It glowed a bright light—one that nearly blinded Jawar—but he did not dare let the magnificent sword fall. The light vanished and the two stared at each other in silence for a few beats. Then, Merlin found the courage to speak.

"How are you still alive?"

Chapter 9:

The Magi Creators

There were few times in Merlin's life that he had been genuinely surprised, and this was one of those times.

In the middle of his cottage, stood a young boy with gentle eyes and a curious look on his face. Merlin did not think he realized that he was wielding perhaps the most powerful weapon on the face of the earth. The boy's eyes flickered between Merlin and the cursed blade, and Merlin could sense that he was struggling to hold it up. The weight was heavy for a young man, so that was not a shock to the sorcerer. It was the fact that he was holding it at all that surprised him.

"You should be dead," Merlin said, when the boy did not answer his question. "What you're holding, it's—"

"Excalibur," he interrupted. "Yes, I know. I did my research before coming here tonight."

Merlin blinked a few times. Was he dreaming? He must be, for there was no way the teen standing before him also knew about the sword's existence. What were the chances of the Djinn sending four bandits to come to steal it with no success, and the boy walking right in, finding it no less, and living to tell the tale?

"How did you know where to find it?" Merlin asked.

A part of him wondered if the Djinn was controlling him like he had the others. He needed to be careful to not reveal any incriminating information that might lead that wicked man straight to him.

"I saw you pulling it out of the stone the other day," he admitted.

With trembling arms, he twisted his body and placed the sword back onto the ancient fabric before taking a seat on the edge of the mattress. A few beads of sweat dripped off of his forehead as he leaned forward and breathed in and out through his nose.

"Where?"

"In the forest. I was taking a walk to get to know the kingdom a little better when I strayed too far from the marketplace. I thought that I had heard something, and I hid behind a tree, and that's when I saw you."

"Interesting," Merlin mused. Taking one of the candlesticks from the table, he dragged the solitary chair in front of the boy and sat down. Reaching over, he pulled the end table beside his bed closer and placed the candlestick on top of it, giving him more light. "I need to see your hands."

"Why?" the boy asked.

"You broke into my home in the middle of the night and attempted to steal something of great value,"

Merlin warned. "I get to ask the questions around here, not you. Now, remove your gloves."

Reluctantly, and perhaps as slowly as he could, the boy removed his gloves. Merlin took them forcefully and placed them closer to the candle to get a good look. There was not a single black mark on either of his hands. They looked exactly as hands should. Tilting his head to the side, Merlin ran the tips of his fingers over the palms and noticed that the boy did not have a single callous.

"You are of high blood," Merlin declared, "but you don't look like King Castilian's son."

"That's because I am not. I'm Prince Jawar Al Naseem of Raimore."

"It's a pleasure to meet you, Prince Jawar." Merlin raised an eyebrow before letting go of his hands. Jawar retracted his arms close to his body, but did not shift away from the sorcerer, even under his heavy gaze.

"How could you tell I wasn't poor?" Jawar asked.

"Firstly, you don't have a worker's hands. Your skin is soft, and your face is rounder, meaning that you don't ever go hungry, and you wear fine clothes. Plus..." He pointed to the pin on his collar—the one that was the symbol of the Castilian family. "Only royals wear those."

Jawar leaned back on his hands and smirked. Merlin had never expected a thief to feel so comfortable in a stranger's home, especially one they intended to steal from. It was rather unusual, but there was something about the young prince that intrigued him. He felt an otherworldly connection, a tether one might say, binding them together. It could not be a coincidence.

"I must admit, they were very wrong about you," he said.

Merlin's eyebrows pinched together. "They?"

"The townspeople. I asked them about the strange man who lives in the forest. They said you were odd, but friendly. I had expected you to be a bit feebleminded, but that's hardly the case. You're observant, and based on the number of books in this cottage, I'd say you're intelligent enough to read. But I do have a question if that's alright."

"Go on," Merlin urged. "I'll allow only one, so choose wisely."

"If you're a sorcerer, one who has magical powers, and have all of these ancient artifacts at your disposal, including Excalibur..." He placed his bare hand against the blade, which glowed for a fraction of a second before returning to its natural color. "Why are you living in a place like this?"

Merlin gnawed on the inside of his cheek to try to stop himself from smirking. The prince, despite his age, knew a great deal about the world around him. He would have to tread carefully. But, luckily, by the sounds of it, he did not speak like the others who were being controlled by the Djinn.

"I'm curious to know your theories," Merlin said. "Care for some tea? I just went to the well to brew some myself. You're welcome to a cup."

"Alright," Jawar agreed. "But I can't stay for long. They don't normally do bed checks, but I'd rather be there if they did."

Merlin stood up from the chair and went to the little fireplace in the corner of the cottage to start boiling some water. There was something about the young boy that ignited something in Merlin's heart. Perhaps he was part of the prophecy that the Djinn had mentioned. Was he a magic wielder? Could he be? But the more important question he kept circling back to was could the lad be trusted?

Once the water boiled, Merlin was quick to make two cups of tea. He handed one to Jawar before moving his chair back to give the young prince his space. Now that he knew that the boy was not in any immediate danger from holding Excalibur, he felt no need to hover over him like he was going to die at any moment.

"So, tell me, why do you suspect I'm all the way out here instead of in the city?" Merlin questioned.

"I feel it's rather obvious, now that I've had time to think about it." Jawar's eyes glanced down at the blade sitting next to him casually on the bed. If he only knew how many people died trying to get that sword to Merlin. "You're hiding something."

"I'm hiding many things." Merlin nodded. "Things you could not think of, even in your wildest dreams."

"I read a book in the castle library!" Jawar blurted. "I know some things. I recognize some of the artifacts, and I would bet that one or two of the books in this cottage have a list of spells in them. What I want to know is why the sword was stuck in the stone and how you were able to pull it out."

"Well, to answer the easiest question, I used magic to retrieve it," Merlin explained. "A simple spell, really, but that's beside the point. The other, more complicated one, is that it traveled here with me, from the past. However, we were separated when I arrived in Taviel, and it has been lost for months. When did you say you arrived in the kingdom?"

"The day that I saw you in the forest," Jawar confirmed. "Why?"

Merlin scratched at the top of his head, but did not answer the prince's question. It was too big of a coincidence to not mean anything. What were the chances of him stumbling upon Excalibur, having walked down that same path for months and simply missing it? Or did it appear precisely when Jawar arrived in Taviel? As illogical as it sounded, the fact that he was able to wield it must only mean one thing.

"Before I tell you what I'm about to, I need to know why you intended to steal it. Were you going to sell it?"

"No," Jawar scoffed. "It's far too valuable to be sold for mere coins. Besides, I have as much money as I'll ever need. I had hoped that it would help my, uh, situation."

"You'll have to be more specific than that," Merlin pried. "We have to learn to trust each other, if we're going to be sharing our darkest secrets."

"Fine," Jawar conceded. "I'm here on political business on behalf of King Umar. Our kingdoms have been feuding for generations, and both have seen many hardships over the years. But my father and King Castilian came to an arrangement. I was sent to Taviel as a token of truce, a peacekeeper if you will, to learn from his family until I'm 18 years old. If everything goes according to plan, our countries will form an alliance once more."

"I don't mean to offend, Your Grace," Merlin grinned, "but you look a long way from 18."

"Yes, I'm only 13. I am to live here for five years."

"And how does Excalibur play into all this?"

"I overheard a conversation between King Castilian and his son, Prince Darrow, the other night. He said that my father was at the beginning stages of assembling an army, and that can only mean one thing."

"He's preparing for war," Merlin offered.

"Exactly. I was hoping that the sword might be able to prevent that from happening. I'm not entirely sure what it does, or how it could help, but I felt like I had to do something. I don't want to see either of our kingdoms fall."

"You're an honorable young man, I'll give you that. Excalibur is the most powerful weapon to have ever existed. Its magic defies the very laws of nature, and it can lay waste to this entire kingdom if used by a strong enough sorcerer... which reminds me, are you a magic wielder, Jawar?"

Merlin tilted his head and studied the young prince's twisted expression. Based on that alone, he assumed a hard no. But that did not make any sense. The blade is cursed, or rather protected, depending on who touches it.

"Of course not!" he proclaimed. "I had only thought that it was a myth until I arrived here. Even now, it's hard to believe."

"Excalibur is cursed. Surely you read that in your little book from the library," Merlin stated. "Any normal man should have—no, has—died from a single touch. But you held it for minutes and yet, here you sit, unharmed. There is only one explanation, and that is that you are the blood of one of the three Magi creators. Perhaps a far descendant, since your family has not told you about being a magic wielder, but it runs in your veins, nonetheless. That's the only reason you were able to touch it without facing your demise."

"So, you are as well? A descendant of one of the Magic creators?"

"We're not talking about me. We're talking about you." Merlin redirected the question. Sipping on his tea, he made a disgusted face, as it had gone stone cold. "If you truly wish to use Excalibur to bring peace between the two kingdoms, you need to work on your skills as a sorcerer. But before you say yes, you must know, magic is not something to take lightly. If used for sinful reasons, it can easily corrupt your entire soul. Only those with pure hearts and strong wills can harness its true power."

"I am my land's only hope. I must do this, whatever it takes. I'm prepared, if you would be willing to teach me."

"We'll do a trial. I don't want to be held responsible for a prince's life," Merlin declared. "There's so much you have yet to learn; wicked forces that seek the sword to exploit its power, dangerous spells, and ferocious beasts that hide within these borders. Are you ready to unlock all of these secrets, even if it takes you down a different path? Once you agree to give yourself to the power of magic, it'll change your life forever."

Jawar looked down at Excalibur, his eyes appreciating it momentarily. Merlin shifted awkwardly in his seat, unsure of what to do if the young prince suddenly burst into tears. But the moment passed, and he held his chin high, placing a hand over his heart.

"I want to do this," he declared.

"Alright," Merlin said. "We start tomorrow. Just know, it won't be easy. I'm going to push you to be the best, perhaps even better than me."

Chapter 10:

Threats from Taviel

It had been weeks since King Umar had seen his only son, and he was not afraid to admit that there was a permanent hole in his heart—one that would never be filled until the day Jawar returned home to Raimore. He knew that sending him to Taviel as a token of truce was the only way to ensure peace between their two kingdoms, but he wished deep down that he did not have to go. Umar was jealous of his brother in that he was going to watch his son grow up. He would get to see him become a young man during his formidable years. Maybe he would even fall in love while in Taviel. He could not know. All he knew was that if he did, his parents were not going to be there to witness it.

"Darling," King Umar called out for his wife. He stepped into the sitting room of their bedchambers, knowing that she had hidden herself inside. "Are you awake?"

"Sadly, yes, though I do not wish to be," Queen Jacia said quietly from the other room. "Why have you returned so quickly? Surely you have some royal business to attend to."

Umar placed a hand over his heart and sighed. He did not like knowing that his wife was so heartbroken. While it had been difficult for him to bear the absence of their son, his mother was barely able to control her emotions. She had been acting as if he were gone forever, and that they had buried him and would never see him again. Umar had tried his best to get her to see reason, but deep down, he knew that she resented both him and Hakim. They had decided without consulting her beforehand, and now, she has to go years without seeing her only son for more than a few short days at a time, if at all.

"Your lady's maid informed me that you turned away your breakfast again," Umar said, as he stepped into their private rooms.

His wife was tucked beneath their blankets, not even out of her sleeping gown. Over the last few weeks, she had barely finished a meal, and her face was beginning to get significantly thinner. On most nights, she stayed awake crying, and only when King Umar had the maids brew her a sleeping draught, would she manage to fall asleep. The castle was starting to fall apart without its queen present, but Umar had no idea what to do. He could not force her to go about her duties, as it would break his heart to do so. But they could not continue on like this for the next five years.

"I was not hungry," Jacia sighed. "I hope you didn't come all this way just to check on me."

Umar sat down on the edge of the mattress and gently stroked his wife's cheek. Her chin trembled, and it did not take long before tears started to fall. He pulled her in close, and she grasped at his vest and sobbed into his chest. They stayed like that for a few minutes, where Umar rubbed gently rubbed her back and rocked her gently.

"Tell me what I can do, my love," Umar pleaded. "I cannot bear to see you like this anymore."

"All I want is my son," Jacia cried. "But that is impossible. It is the price we must pay for ruling an entire kingdom."

"Why don't you write to him?" Umar suggested. "Tell him all about your days and what you have been doing, even if you have to fib a little bit so he does not worry about you. Write to him as if he were sitting right beside you. I'll have one of my men ride out tomorrow to Taviel and deliver it himself if I must. King Castilian and I correspond quite frequently. It'll arrive before you know it."

"What if he does not write back?" she sniffled. "I fear my heart would break into a thousand pieces."

"Jawar loves you." Umar grabbed his wife by the face so that she had no choice but to look at him. "He is our son, and he would never do anything to hurt your feelings. I'll bet he is waiting to hear from you first so that he does not look too eager."

"Do you believe so?"

For the first time in weeks, Jacia's eyes had a twinkle in them. It was subtle, but it was enough for Umar to have hope that his wife could heal from this trauma.

"Of course I do!" he chimed. "Now, get out of this bed so that the maids can give it a proper cleaning. Put on a gown, even if it's just a plain dress, and go sit in your study and write a letter to our son. Tell him that I love him and miss him."

With Umar's help, Jacia slipped out of bed and stepped in front of her wardrobe to find what she was going to wear. While she was not looking, Umar knocked on the servant's entrance door and his wife's maid entered promptly.

"Good morning, Your Majesty," she greeted. "Can I help dress you?"

"Yes, please." Jacia waved her over. "And when you're done, can you fetch me something to eat from the kitchen? I'm absolutely famished! I'll be in my study for the afternoon, and then afterward, perhaps you and I can go for a stroll in the courtyard. I think I could do with some fresh air."

"That sounds like a wonderful idea." Her maid smiled.

The maid got to work on untying the back of the queen's nightgown and Umar kissed his wife's cheek. "I'll be back in a few hours, my darling. I just have some business to discuss with Hakim. Perhaps we'll eat dinner together in our sitting room—nothing too formal—I want you to be comfortable."

"I think we can manage that. Tell the chef that I want chicken. Oh, and those little pastries that Jawar loves so much, if he has the time."

"Anything you want, you shall have. Just say the word, and it shall be done."

"Does that mean you'll bring me flowers?" Jacia teased. "I would not refuse some new jewelry either."

"There's my wife that I missed so much," Umar said. He kissed her once more, and then gave her a few more after that for good measure. "I'll see you soon."

***

King Umar sat perched at the end of the throne room table, busying himself with some invitations to a few upcoming royal events to pass the time.

Normally, his wife took care of such matters, as her handwriting was impeccable and Umar's was, well, legible at best, but he did not want to overwhelm her. This was the first day in weeks that she had agreed to get out of bed, and he was not about to upset her over some invitations. Besides, she had an important letter to focus on.

While Umar was pouring wax at the fold of the page, Hakim burst through the doors. Startled, Umar spilled it all over himself and the table. He hissed as the hot wax burned his forearm.

"Hakim," Umar growled, scrambling to place his seal before it solidified on the paper completely. "What is the meaning of this?"

"I have received word from King Castilian," his brother began.

Waving his hands at the guards, they shut the doors promptly, and Umar's stomach churned. While his younger brother had a bit of a flair for the dramatic, he never did so unless there was truly a crisis.

"And? What news of Jawar? Are they sending him back? Has he done something to offend them? Oh, I knew this was a bad idea."

"Relax, Your Majesty," Hakim sighed. "Jawar is safe."

He took the seat closest to the king and laid out an envelope on the table. The seal was barely legible, as Hakim had already opened and read it beforehand, but Umar could just make out the seal. It belonged to King Castilian.

"If Jawar is not in any immediate danger, why rush in here like this? Can't you see I'm on edge as it is? Jacia has practically been drowning in her tears every single night. There is much to be done and I have little help."

"Just read it," Hakim urged.

Glaring at his brother from beneath his reading glasses, Umar yanked the piece of paper from the table and began to read out loud.

"His Majesty King Umar and Her Majesty Queen Jacia, it brings me no pleasure to write you this, but I feel as if there is nothing left for me to do. While I too felt like it had been a good idea at the time to send Jawar to Taviel to promote peace between the two kingdoms, I fear it has done everything but. He has informed me that you are preparing an army to stage an attack while we are in a truce, and that sending him here was only a ruse created to distract me. It seems that this burden was too much for the young boy to share. While I appreciate his honesty, I'm afraid I cannot trust him any longer. We have had to take some precautions to keep our kingdom, and more importantly my children, safe. What kind of man sends his son to execute another boy? I did not realize you were training young assassins. Let me be clear when I say this—should he succeed, although I sincerely doubt he will, given what we've done with him—you will face the same fate as I. The only difference will be that I still have another son to assume my throne, while Jawar is the sole heir of Raimore. I hope you choose your next actions wisely, as they may very well be your last. Cordially, King Castilian."

King Umar read the letter several times more, but silently. He dissected every last word, hoping that this was all some sort of sick joke. What had Jawar done? This did not sound like the son he had raised from infancy. Surely, there had to have been some misunderstanding. Perhaps he and the other prince were simply playing, and someone overheard their conversation.

Jawar was not a murderer—he would never intentionally inflict harm upon another living thing. Even in the last few years, when Umar had brought up the idea of him one day leading an army, Jawar had been hesitant. He always said that he wanted to find another way—one that did not result in violence.

"What have they done with my son?" Umar growled.

He balled up the letter in his fist and squeezed it tight, wishing it would disintegrate into oblivion. He thought about tossing it into the blazing fire behind them, but decided against it. They would need to hold onto this letter as evidence of King Castilian's treacherous words.

"By the sounds of it, he imprisoned him until they could figure out what he plans to do. I don't understand. Jawar was always so gentle and caring growing up. Why would he try to kill Prince Darrow?"

"He wouldn't!" Umar cried. "These are lies, all of it. Jawar knew the importance of this mission, he loves Raimore, and would never jeopardize the state of his kingdom over one child's life."

"Let's not focus on what that wretched man said about your son," Hakim sighed. "What are we going to do about his threats? I can only imagine that he has started to assemble an army as we speak, and is preparing to march through the countryside to attack the city."

Umar leaned back into his seat and rubbed at his temples. After everything they had done to prevent history from repeating itself, they were back to where they had started —feuding over what was likely a bunch of nonsense.

"Right now, we do nothing," Umar decided. His brother pursed his lips at this final verdict, as if he had been wishing for something different. "Until I receive a legitimate declaration of war, I will not be the first to draw a sword. I want peace just as much as they do. My father, and his before him, may have jumped at the chance to fight, but that is not who I am. That is not the kind of man I want my son to be either."

"I see." Hakim gritted his teeth. "Just know, if this decision costs him his life, that is something you will have to live with for the rest of your days. I also do not imagine that his mother would be awfully fond of you if anything were to happen to him."

Umar stood out of his seat and loomed over his baby brother. "Do I detect a hint of a threat beneath those words of yours, Hakim? I could have you imprisoned for treason. I suggest that you learn your place among my ranks. Otherwise, you'll be paying for it with *your* life."

"Apologizes, Your Majesty." Hakim slouched in his chair and lowered his head in submission. "I promise I only had my nephew's best interests at heart. It won't happen again."

"The contents of this letter must stay between the two of us. Do I make myself clear? I do not want Jacia worrying about this, not in her state."

"My lips are sealed."

Chapter 11:

The Blacksmith's Daughter

Prince Jawar feared that something bad was going to happen when King Castilian began dismissing him from his regular duties.

It had started a few weeks after he started training with Merlin late at night. At first, Jawar had assumed that the king found out where he had been sneaking off to when he was supposed to be in his bed sleeping. But when no one mentioned Merlin or the study of magic, he realized that it was something much bigger. Sadly, that meant it would also not be an easy fix. Normally, Jawar would shadow King Castilian along with his eldest son, Prince Darrow, just as he had with his father in Raimore. He was even granted permission to sit in on a few meetings with other royals and political members from whom the king sought counsel. Jawar had felt honored, as he had never seen so many gathered in a room before to decide the fate of the kingdom as a whole. Normally, that was only something that his father and uncle did together.

Unfortunately, all of that stopped about a week ago. King Castilian would send servants to his room and say that his attendance was not required and that he had the day off. The only thing he kept consistent in his schedule was his tutoring lessons with Master Tal. Even then, Prince Darrow was no longer present. When Jawar had asked his tutor why that was, he said he was not at liberty to discuss the king's wishes with a Raimore son.

Jawar felt completely and utterly defeated. He wanted to ask what he had done wrong, if he had offended the family in some way, but he was afraid to bring it up. What if he made things worse? What if he was overthinking the situation and they laughed at his concerns? The last thing he wanted to do was to make a fool of himself, so instead, he kept his mouth shut and his head down. He did what he was told and stayed away when they did not want him around. Without any family to offer guidance or protection in Taviel, that was all he could do.

The only upside to King Castilian shutting Jawar out was the fact that he now had more free time during the day. Most of the time, he spent it at the cottage with Merlin, but this afternoon the sorcerer had said he had matters to attend to, and that they would resume their lessons come nightfall. So, Jawar headed for the only other place in the kingdom that he felt safe—the blacksmith's shop.

Neo and Rosa had become Jawar's only other companions in the royal city. He secretly wondered if he were also burdening them with his friendship, but they had never discouraged his visits. Rosa had even offered to teach him a few of the basics of forging weapons.

Zigzagging through the busy streets of the marketplace, Jawar spotted Rosa's braids from afar. Standing just outside her shop, she was deep in conversation with a gentleman who looked a few years older than her. A hint of jealousy pricked the back of Jawar's neck, but he quickly dismissed it with a shake of his head.

The two of them glanced at Jawar as he approached. Upon further inspection, the young man looked like a recruit for the royal guard. He wore the Castilian colors, along with a few pieces of armor. In his hands, was a freshly made sword, one of Neo's finest.

"Greetings, Your Grace," the man bowed. "I did not think I would have the opportunity to speak with you face to face."

Rosa scrunched up her nose in confusion. She had admitted that she did not see Jawar as one of those snobbish royals who never stopped to say hello to anyone. In fact, she said if it were not for his garments, he could easily blend in with the common folk, based on his personality alone.

"Prince Jawar is very humble," Rosa stated. "He does not abuse his status."

"Oh." The guard nodded. "I'm Henry, by the way. I've just been assigned to the night duty in the castle. Perhaps we'll cross paths every now and then."

"I do enjoy an evening stroll when the weather permits," Jawar replied. "It helps me to fall asleep."

"Well, I should be getting back inside." Rosa pointed her thumb over her shoulder toward the shop, her other hand grazing Jawar's forearm in the process. "The prince here needs to collect his order."

"Right. Well, tell your father thanks again for the blade. I know it's required of a guard to have a weapon, but I still appreciate it."

"He lives to service His Majesty." Rosa smiled.

Henry bowed to Jawar once more before retreating into the crowd, which seemed to part just for him. They watched him disappear around the corner before Rosa visibly deflated.

"It's the one thing I hate about this job," she groaned.

"What?" Jawar asked, still staring at the space that Henry occupied only moments ago. His entire body felt tense, and he had not realized that he had been flexing his muscles until he allowed his body to relax.

"Being polite."

She waved her hands as if it were an atrocious notion that she had to be kind to the customers. Looping her hand around his arm, she practically yanked him back inside the scorching shop. Jawar immediately discarded his cloak and vest, stripping down to just his tunic and trousers. Even that, he unbuttoned so only the bottom was together, allowing his skin to breathe.

"Good afternoon, Jawar," Neo greeted from the forge. "How are things in the castle?"

"Same as always," Jawar frowned. "I wish I knew what I could do to make them like me."

"If they cannot see how wonderful you are, they are fools," Rosa stated.

Wrapping her apron around her waist, she got to work assisting her father with the next order. Jawar slid into the high stool at the table just off to the side, watching in wonderment. He found the entire process of forging a weapon absolutely fascinating. He was perfectly content with sitting quietly and watching them work.

"So, where's this special order of mine?" Jawar asked.

Rosa's cheeks flushed, but she quickly recovered. "Oh, I just said that so he would go away. You know how I hate small talk."

"Yes," Jawar nodded, a grin tugging at the corners of his lips. "I'm well aware."

"Say, are you busy this evening for supper?" Neo asked. "I'm making Rosa's favorite—bean stew. There will be plenty to go around, and I thought it might be a nice change of scenery."

"Father," Rosa hissed. "Why would Jawar want to give up plates of the castle's finest meals to come and dine with us?"

"I'd love to," Jawar said. "Just as long as it doesn't interfere with my commitment with Merlin. He wants to meet me at nightfall for our daily training."

Neo's nose twitched at the mention of the sorcerer, but he did not say anything about it. "Of course not. In fact, he will be stopping by around that time anyway, so it'll be convenient for you both."

"Wonderful." Jawar slipped off the stool and headed for the door. "I'll be back in a few hours then. I should try to make some effort in the castle, so that they do not cast me out completely."

He meant it as a joke, but deep down, he wondered if that was what the king had intended to do all along. Jawar would not know who to turn to if that happened. Perhaps he would seek refuge with Merlin and live in the dingy old cottage for the rest of his days.

***

Jawar stood outside of the blacksmith's shop with a bundle of wildflowers in his hand.

He had never been invited to anyone's home before. He was not entirely familiar with proper etiquette, but his mother had always mentioned that it was nice to bring something for the table, and flowers were the first thing that came to his mind.

After he was standing there for what felt like a lifetime, Rosa opened the shop door and nearly took Jawar's breath away. She was not covered in soot, nor was her hair tied up out of her face, but instead, flowed in ringlets around her shoulders. She smelled of lilacs and wore a dress that he had never seen before.

"How long have you been standing there?" she asked, tilting her head to the side and looking at him from the boots up.

"I—I just got here."

"Oh." She blinked. "Well, come on. The soup's going to get cold if we stay out here any longer."

"You live inside the blacksmith shop?"

"Beneath it," Rosa confirmed. "It's a small house, but it suits us fine. I don't have any other siblings, so it's just Father and me."

"And your mother?" Jawar asked, but based on the flicker of pain in Rosa's eyes, he wished that he could take it back.

"She died when I was young. I don't remember her all that much, but my father has plenty of stories about her if you're curious to know. He'll talk about her all night, if you let him."

Jawar nodded and left it at that. He followed her through the blacksmith shop, which was still hot, but not nearly as bad as it was during the day. In the back room there was a staircase, and he could hear Neo singing faintly. Fiddling with the collar of his tunic,

Jawar stepped into their tiny home and was surprised by the amount of decor that covered the walls.

There were paintings, shelves of books and trinkets, candles, and toys that looked like they were from Rosa's childhood. The main room had two beds separated by a partition, and Jawar assumed that it doubled as their bedchambers. Just down the hall was their kitchen and eating area, where Neo hovered over a wood-burning stove, which held a massive pot of bubbling stew in the center.

"Welcome to our home!" Neo chimed. "We're so pleased to have you."

"I brought these." Jawar shoved the flowers into Rosa's hands, and she giggled a bit before taking them gingerly. "My mother always said it was a nice gesture to bring a small gift to the host."

"She raised a good man." Neo smiled. "There should be a vase in that top cupboard, Rosa. Put some water in it and we'll put it on the table."

"What you are cooking smells delicious."

Jawar stood beside the blacksmith and looked inside the pot. He had tasted a lot of different meals in his lifetime, but something about this dish felt special. The kitchen staff in the castles were required to feed them and the rest of the royal family, but Neo was not obligated to share his food with him. He had chosen to do so, of his own accord. That meant the world to Jawar.

"Rosa dear, the bowls. Otherwise, we'll be eating straight out of the pot."

"It wouldn't be the first time," Rosa snickered, handing each of them a clay pot. Jawar admired their uniqueness. They had chips in the edges and appeared to be hand-painted, but he thought they were beautiful.

The three of them each served themselves a ladle of stew and gathered at the small table in the kitchen. They ate in silence for a few minutes as Neo and Rosa were too occupied with shoveling the stew into their mouths to chat. He imagined that, after working so many hours, a person would feel famished.

He was perfectly content with not speaking at all and then Neo cleared his throat. "So, Jawar, tell us, are you enjoying your time in Taviel?"

Rosa glared at her father from across the table, as if trying to speak to him without using words.

"Other than the fact that I think the king hates me, it's pretty nice. It's a whole new experience, that's for sure. I never got to do things like this in Raimore. I was pretty much locked in the castle."

"I weep for you," Rosa smirked, before kicking him gently with the toe of her boot. "We're humbled you agreed to grace us with your presence."

"What Rosa means is that we're happy to call you a friend. There are not many kids in the market district of Rosa's age, so I'm sure she's grateful to have you around."

"It's true." She nodded. "I think Prince Darrow has spoken fewer than a dozen words to me."

"He's not so bad," Jawar sighed. "It might sound odd, but we're taught from a young age to try to separate ourselves from the working families. If we form bonds, it makes it harder to decide their fates."

"So why do you do it then?" Rosa inquired.

"I'm not a real prince here, at least not in their eyes. I'm free to do whatever I want."

"Like practicing magic." Neo placed his spoon down beside his bowl and folded his hands on the table. There was something in his eyes. Jawar could not quite place it, but it seemed as if he somewhat disapproved of Jawar's nighttime activities.

"Do you not like Merlin?"

"Merlin, despite his quirks, is a good man. He's one of the few magic wielders that I have met who do not use it for malicious purposes."

Jawar nearly choked on the stew in his mouth. "You know other sorcerers?"

"Certainly. They're not as rare as you might think. You just have to know where to look."

"Does Merlin know?"

"Magic wielders can sense one another," Neo began. His voice was thick, and he refused to meet Jawar's gaze. "It's as if they are all connected by tiny, invisible threads. It's the magic binding them together, always and forever."

"I wonder if that's how I was able to find him," Jawar mumbled. "Merlin thinks I'll be a powerful sorcerer one day if I practice. He says it comes naturally to me."

"Just be careful," Neo warned. "Magic can be dangerous if not used correctly." He tilted his head to the side for a few seconds, before picking up his spoon again. "He's here."

Seconds later, Merlin descended the stairs and walked into the kitchen area, leaning his weight on the doorframe. "I've come bearing gifts. Where do you want them, Neo?"

"Just on my desk in the other room." Neo pointed over his shoulder and gave the sorcerer a nod of gratitude. "I guess that means you'll be heading off now?"

"Yes," Merlin answered for Jawar. "We have lots of work to do. I have a special mission that I need your help with."

Jawar brushed his hand against Rosa's and thanked Neo for his hospitality. "I'll see you tomorrow."

"Take care, Jawar, and know you're welcome here anytime," Neo offered. "You're one of us now."

Jawar was grateful that his back was turned so they could not see his foolish smile. Even though he would one day be King of Raimore, it felt nice to belong to this group of people. Deep down, he did not know if he wanted to be king, after all. Since arriving in Taviel, he felt as if he were going down a different path, one that was leading him farther away from his duties as a prince.

Chapter 12:

The Hunt for Artifacts

Merlin had the perfect solution to distract the little prince from the thoughts that plagued his mind.

He would never openly admit that he could feel the ache in his heart, or that his lack of sleep was beginning to affect his ability to control magic. The last thing he wanted to do was make Jawar feel uncomfortable or embarrassed. But it was not just Jawar who was riddled with tension. Merlin felt it everywhere—all over the royal city.

The guards were affected the most. They knew something. Perhaps King Castilian had ordered them to keep a watchful eye on anything suspicious, but the darkness from their secrets and misery was practically oozing from their bodies. That was the thing about magic—it concentrated on a person's energy, their soul, and their entire being. Even if they were not sorcerers themselves, Merlin could still sense their emotions, although they were a bit more clouded and gray than those of his fellow wielders.

The tension was nearing its peak in Taviel, and as much as Merlin wanted to focus on the Djinn and whatever evil plans that he had brewing in the past, he knew that Jawar needed his help.

Most of all, the young boy just needed a break from everything he had resting on his shoulders. All he ever talked about was duty, honor, and responsibility. Even though he was a prince, he was still a youth and had plenty of years left before he should have had to worry about any of those things.

Merlin resented Jawar's father and King Castilian for dragging Jawar into the middle of their childish feuds. He should have never been their token of truce.

Sadly, despite Merlin's abilities, he could not change the past. Nor could he run from it, as the Djinn had made abundantly clear, which was why tracking down ancient artifacts would benefit them both.

Merlin sensed Jawar approaching the cottage before he even stepped up onto the porch. With a flick of his wrist, the hatch unlocked, and the door swung open just as the boy came into view.

"I still don't know how you do that," Jawar mused as he walked inside.

Rubbing the bottom of his boots on the rug in front of the door, he slipped his pack off of his shoulders, and it hit the floor with a loud thud. Merlin cocked an eyebrow and eyed the leather sack.

"Are you bringing everything you own?" he teased.

Jawar stuck his tongue out at the sorcerer and took a seat on a second chair that Merlin had purchased from the market. He helped himself to a cup of tea that Merlin had just brewed for their travels. He was just finishing up the last of their food rations and they would be heading out soon enough.

"I've never been on an adventure before," Jawar admitted. "I didn't know what to pack."

"Normally, I would advise packing *lightly,*" Merlin mused. "A few extra garments in case it gets cold, or you get wet, food, a weapon—not that you'll need any with me around. I do hope you were clever enough to not pack any coins with you."

"I'm not a fool," Jawar scoffed. "I just brought some journals and books, you know, to document everything. I don't want to come home and forget something important."

"If it's important, you won't forget." Merlin tapped the side of his head and smirked. "What does King Castilian think of your little excursion with the city's sorcerer anyway?"

"Right. About that." Jawar stood up from his chair and proceeded to pace around the cottage. "I didn't exactly tell him. But I did leave him a note saying that I'd be back by tomorrow."

Merlin clicked his tongue as he wrapped up the last of the bread and cheese before stuffing them into his bag.

He was not particularly happy about the idea of the king not knowing where the young ward was at all times, but there was little to do about it now. Besides, from what Jawar had said about their bond lately, Merlin predicted that he would not even notice that he was gone.

"I'm sure it'll be fine," Merlin said. "Besides, we'll only be gone for the day. It's half a day's walk from here, if I've calculated it right, and then we'll camp for the night and head back in the morning."

"Shall we?" Jawar grinned from ear to ear as he bounced out onto the front porch. Perhaps bringing a young boy on a quest like this was not such a good idea after all.

"We're heading east. I'll let you take the lead for the first little while," Merlin decided. "I'll need to focus my magic on tracking down the artifact's exact location."

"Fine, but if we get lost it's your fault for leaving it in my hands."

***

"Do you remember the light spell I taught you?"

"Yes," Jawar said. "It's burned into my mind forever."

"Light our path. It's getting dark and we're so deep in the forest that what little daylight we have left won't pass through the leaves."

They had been traveling east for hours, and not once had Jawar strayed from the correct path. Merlin wondered if he could subconsciously sense the artifact's energy, similar to how Merlin tracked it down. That was the only explanation. It was not like the boy was a skilled explorer. He had never left Raimore's city walls in the 13 years he had lived there, and he had never been in this part of Taviel before.

No, this was pure magical instinct. The more he worked and trained with Merlin, the more he tapped into his true potential. It was fascinating to watch him become a little mage.

Holding his hands palm up, Jawar recited the spell under his breath. Instantly, two glowing orbs hovered just above his hands, lighting the dense path ahead. Critters scampered through the forest, startled by the bright lights.

Spotting a clearing just up ahead, Merlin knew that they were nearly to their destination. They had made good time, and once he had the artifact in his possession, they would set up camp and get some rest. He sensed that Jawar was getting tired from all the walking, assuming he had never traveled as far in his life.

"See that well?" Merlin pointed over Jawar's shoulder, just north of where they were standing. "That's it."

"A well?" Jawar questioned. "I thought we were looking for an artifact, not a landmark."

"It's in the well," Merlin explained. "You'll see."

Jawar picked up his pace then, and Merlin had to take longer strides just to keep up. It was not long before they stepped out onto padded grass, and Merlin's legs felt instant relief from climbing over fallen trees and overgrown roots for the past few hours. Jawar huffed and sank to his knees, his pack falling from his back and landing in the soft grass.

"Now I know why you said to pack lightly."

"Don't say I didn't tell you so," Merlin snickered. "At least you will know for next time."

Jawar's eyes lit up with excitement. "You mean we will go on more adventures like this one?"

"I don't see why not."

Merlin circled the ancient well twice, examining its condition. The last thing he needed was to lean his body weight on it and have it crumble beneath his weight. Determining it would hold its structure, Merlin peered down into the well, only to find nothing but darkness. That did not come as a shock. He assumed that the well had not been functioning in at least one hundred years.

"I feel it," Jawar whispered.

He stood next to Merlin and raised his arm up, showing that the hairs were standing upright, just the same as Merlin's were. The energy in this artifact was strong, and he was grateful that they had been the ones to find it, not someone else.

"Close your eyes," Merlin instructed. "Try and call it up. Use all your senses, even the ones you didn't know existed."

Jawar nibbled on his bottom lip and nodded. Placing his hands out over the open hole, he closed his eyes and squeezed them as tightly as he could. Merlin watched attentively, and after a minute or two, he saw them.

The Dice of Destiny.

They existed in Merlin's time. He wondered if they had remained in the well all of this time, and apparently, no one had found their hiding spot. As they hovered at eye level, Jawar snatched them before they could fall back down the well.

"Are these what I think they are?" Jawar beamed.

Merlin assumed that he must have read about them in the sorcery book he found in the library. Carefully, he handed them over to Merlin, who placed them into a small leather pouch, where they would remain safe.

"Yes, and they're very powerful so we must be careful."

"Don't you want to try them out?"

Merlin scratched at the side of his beard and drummed his lips with his fingers. He would be lying if he said he was not curious to learn about what the future held for him, but at the same time, he knew it was not his right to know. The sorcerer who created this artifact was a wicked man, quite like the Djinn, and Merlin was a firm believer that it was not right to try to change fate's design. If he were to find out something that he did not like, he might not be able to resist the temptation to forge a new path. Fate existed for a reason—he was not going to mess up someone else's life because he did not like his own.

"The future has already been decided. There's no point in finding out sooner. No good could come from it."

"I don't understand," Jawar confessed. "Why did we come all this way to find them if you're just going to hide them from the rest of the world."

"I do this to keep mankind safe!" Merlin raised his voice for the first time at Jawar. It was not that he was upset or angry with the little prince, but it was a complicated matter, and one that he did not know if he could ever understand.

"I'm sorry I asked."

"It's fine. Listen, you stay here and set up camp, collect some firewood, and set out the sleeping mats. I'm going to go collect some fresh water. There's a stream not far from here."

Merlin walked off before Jawar could object to his duties. It was true, they needed fresh water for the night, but Merlin just needed a minute or two to clear his mind. The more he brought Jawar into the light of the magic world, the more danger he was putting him in. If the Djinn ever found out about his natural abilities, there was no telling to what lengths he would go, to travel to this time.

Spotting the creek, Merlin retrieved his wine sack from his belt and dipped it into the water. Seconds later, an ear-piercing screech disrupted the birds nestled in the treetops above.

"Jawar!" Merlin's heart stopped.

Abandoning his belongings at the river bank, he tore through the forest, fearing what he would find when he reached the well. He heard a group of voices as he neared, as well as Jawar pleading for mercy. Storming the clearing, the little prince was surrounded by five men who had cornered him against the well.

His fists were up as if he was prepared to fight them all on his own. It seemed that they already had a little tousle, as Jawar's nose was bleeding, and one of the men's eyes was swollen. He must have landed at least one punch.

"Give us your coin purse," one of the men growled. "It's not worth your life."

"I told you already, I don't have anything on me!" Jawar shouted.

The man hit Jawar in the face again, and he let out a tiny yelp. Merlin had seen enough. Merlin screamed at the top of his lungs, and all five of them dropped like flies. Jawar covered his ears with his hands, curling up as far against the well as he could.

Merlin raced across the clearing and cupped Jawar's face in his hands to assess the damage. He did not think that his nose was broken, which was a good sign, but he would certainly have bruises for the next few days.

"Are they dead?" Jawar whispered.

"No," Merlin said. "But they'll be knocked out for a few hours at least. Their memory will be foggy too, so they shouldn't bother us again. Come now, I know you're probably tired, but we should find a new place to camp for the night."

Jawar, unable to form any words about what had just transpired, nodded. He allowed Merlin to tuck his hand beneath his shoulders, guiding him through the unconscious bodies that lay at their feet. It had been a long time since Merlin used his magic like that. But it had been like second nature when he saw Jawar in danger. While he had only known the young prince for a few weeks, Merlin knew in his heart that he would be willing to die to keep him safe.

Chapter 13:

Arrest Prince Jawar

"What do you mean Prince Jawar is not in his room?"

King Castilian looked at him from the papers on his desk, his left eyebrow shooting up. He found it quite unusual. While they had been distancing themselves from each other over the past several days, not once did Jawar neglect to inform the king that he was leaving the castle for the afternoon. It was always the same. He would come to the council room, where he and Prince Darrow would start their morning duties and, after seeing if they required his assistance, he would inform His Majesty that he was going out into the marketplace.

The guards kept a close eye on where he went and who he spent most of his time with, and so far, nothing too concerning was brought to his attention. He usually went straight to the blacksmith's shop. King Castilian discovered that Neo had a daughter around the same age as Jawar, and so he figured that he had a crush on the girl.

"We've checked everywhere, Your Majesty. He's not in the castle. Master Tal said he did not show up for his lessons, and Prince Darrow did not see him wandering the halls near their rooms. I spoke with the maid who was on duty to clean his bedchambers and she informed me that his bed had not been slept in."

Tea burned King Castilian's nostrils as he nearly choked on his drink. "What! What do you mean he did not sleep in his bed last night? Where is he?"

The guard's skin flushed, and he looked as if he nearly wet himself from the thunder of the king's voice. With trembling hands, he held out a scribbled note. "They found this under his bed. It must have fallen under there from the draft."

He ripped the note out of the guard's hand and turned his back on him. "Dear King Castilian, I could not find you last night, so I hope you will not be inconvenienced when you find this. I've gone out on a little bit of an adventure. It's very important, but I don't want you to worry about me. Merlin has sworn to keep me safe. I should return late tomorrow afternoon. Signed, Prince Jawar."

King Castilian, bubbling with rage, tore the note into little pieces. Half of them fluttered into the fireplace, incinerating immediately. The others drifted to the floor, making the room look as if it had been snowing inside.

"What does it mean, Your Majesty?" the guard asked.

It meant that Castilian's worst fears had come true. The truce was never real. It had all been a ploy—something to keep him distracted while King Umar prepared for war. He may have outsmarted Castilian this time, but what he seemed to forget was that his son and heir remained in his domain. He could do what he pleased with Jawar, and there was nothing any of them could do about it. He just hoped that he was not too late with what he had planned. The letters he had received from Raimore were proof enough that Jawar was indeed a traitor, and no one would object to whatever sentence he levied against him.

"That the Al Naseem's cannot be trusted."

"What will you have me do?"

"Gather 11 of your best soldiers, and prepare my horse as well." He gritted his teeth. "We're going hunting."

***

With King Castilian leading the search party through the woods, it did not take long to find the prince.

As it had said in his note, Merlin was leading the way, and he looked rather surprised to find a horde of Taviel soldiers barreling towards them on horseback.

"What is the meaning of this?" Merlin questioned, using his body as a shield to protect the little traitor from being trampled by two dozen hooves.

"Step out of the way, unless you wish to be locked in chains as well, sorcerer," King Castilian growled.

Sliding off of his horse, he whistled, altering the prison wagon that they had found what they were looking for. "You had us quite fooled, Prince Jawar, I will admit that. I thought you were a peacekeeper, just like my son, but it turns out you're the exact opposite. Your family has been plotting this all along, haven't they? You have been toying with me, spying on me, and sending information back to your father and uncle in Raimore. Well, I'm glad I found out sooner rather than later."

"What—what are you talking about, Your Majesty?" Prince Jawar stuttered. "Whatever it is you think I have done, I swear on my life I'm innocent. I only went out with Merlin to find something he lost, and that's all."

"I can vouch for the boy," Merlin interjected, earning him a nasty glare from the king. "What he says is true."

"If you speak one more time without my permission, I'll cut your tongue from your mouth!" he bellowed. "Know your place or I'll have one of the guards teach it to you. Now stand down. This matter is no longer your concern."

Merlin puffed his chest out, as if ready to fight the king in front of all these people, but Jawar grazed his hand against his forearm, and he snapped out of it. Tears pricked the little prince's eyes, but still, he found the courage to stand in front of his enemy with a brave face.

King Castilian pointed to the two closest guards still on their horses. "You two, I want you to escort Merlin here back to his cottage in the woods. He is not to leave his home until tomorrow morning. I don't want him anywhere near the castle while I interrogate our little friend here."

"Yes, Your Majesty." The guards saluted.

"Run along now, Merlin," King Castilian sneered. "I'll take good care of Jawar, you have my word."

"Why do I feel like your word means nothing right now?" Merlin fumed, before placing both of his hands on Jawar's shoulders. "Be strong, little prince. Remember, this is not your fight, you're just a piece in their little game."

"That's quite enough." One of the guards on foot gave Merlin a little push to get him moving along. "The king's offer still stands."

Just then, the prison wagon mowed down the tall grass and underbrush they were gathered in. One of the guards unlocked the rusted padlock and swung the iron gate all the way open.

"Prince Jawar, you are under arrest for your treachery against Taviel. You will have a fair trial where I will determine whether or not you shall live or die for your crimes. Now, you have two choices. Give yourself up without a struggle, and I'll take this into consideration when we return to the castle, or you can try to run, but know, you will never be able to outrun a dozen horses. Choose wisely."

Without even a flicker of hesitation, he stepped toward King Castilian with both of his arms up in surrender. "I know I've done nothing wrong, you'll see. Do what you must."

With a snap of the king's fingers, two guards jumped into action, one of them twisting the boy's wrists behind his back, and the other locking the chain to secure him in place. With tears streaming down his face, he did not say a single word after that, even as the guards hauled him into the prison wagon and tossed him with no regard for his well-being. It made King Castilian's heart twinge just a little bit.

What if Jawar was telling the truth? What if all this was one big misunderstanding? If it were, and King Umar found out how he had treated his son with such disrespect, surely that would be the final straw and they really would be go to war.

"Just a moment," King Castilian called out to Merlin, and the sorcerer merely looked over his shoulder. "What happened to his face?"

"He tried to fight off five bandits!" Merlin spat. "Somehow, I feel like he might have been better off in that situation than the one he's in right now."

Not allowing King Castilian the satisfaction of having the final word, the sorcerer walked off, with his two escorts trailing behind him on horseback. The king stood there for a moment, watching them go, before turning back to the prison wagon. Jawar had curled himself up into the far corner, with his eyes squeezed shut. His face was bruised, and there was a bit of dried blood beneath his nose. He had a few other cuts here and there on his arms, as if he had run through the forest at full speed and the branches had pierced his flesh. Other than that, he looked as he always did, just a little bit more broken and tired.

"I know when you first arrived here, that I said that we could be friends, and I still believe that could be true. I'm just doing what I think is best for my country. I hope you understand that."

Jawar opened one eye and stared daggers at the king for a few beats before he closed it again. He did not say a single word, and he did not move, not even to readjust himself or get more comfortable. He stayed perfectly still, almost as if he were not even real.

"I'll meet you back at the castle!" he called out to the guard leading the wagon. "Have him brought to the throne room and ensure that neither one of my children are anywhere near it. Do I make myself clear?"

"Yes, Your Majesty."

With that, the search party trudged forward, and King Castilian climbed back into his saddle, praying to the gods that he was not about to make the worst mistake of his life.

***

After pacing outside the throne room for nearly 20 minutes, King Castilian finally found the courage to face his enemy's son.

Jawar knelt in front of the dais with his hands still bound in chains. No one had tended to his wounds, which did not come as a surprise. He had left as Castilian's ward and returned as a prisoner. No one was going to be showing him any form of kindness or affection without the king's approval.

Letting out a deep sigh, the king sat on the edge of his throne, gripping the edges of his arms rests to regain control of his emotions.

"Do you know why you have been placed under arrest, Jawar?"

"Because you think I'm a traitor."

"Are you?"

Jawar's face twisted with disgust. King Castilian tried to act unphased. Perhaps the prince was just a master of deceit.

"Do you think I would have waited this long to show my true colors, Your Majesty? Do you think I would have dined with you and your family, spent hours studying in the library after Master Tal and your son went to bed to learn more about your history, your culture, and your way of life? Do you think I would have done all that if I was a traitor to your country?"

"I don't know," Castilian remarked. "I have no idea to what extent you are willing to go to protect your secrets."

"I don't have any!" Jawar cried. "Merlin asked me to help him find one of his personal belongings and I said yes. You have not wanted me around for some time now. Don't bother denying it. You've suspected me. I don't know why, but you have. That's why you no longer wanted me to shadow you at your political meetings. You were afraid of what I might overhear."

King Castilian contemplated denying all of Jawar's accusations, but they were all true—every last one of them.

"King Umar has started to assemble his soldiers, he's preparing for war, and I want to know how much you know."

"I don't know anything about that. I am only aware of what you told Prince Darrow one night outside of my bedchambers."

The king froze in his seat momentarily, having been caught off guard. That had been a private conversation. He did not know that Jawar had heard it.

"So you have been spying on us."

"No," Jawar groaned. "I was coming back from the library when I heard you two talking. I've been trying everything I can to prevent our two countries from going to war against each other. Please, you must believe me. I don't want this, and I know you don't either."

Standing up, King Castilian stepped down from the dais and clapped his hands twice. "Prince Jawar, you have been found guilty of conspiring against the King of Taviel, and for that, you will be locked in the dungeons."

Four guards dragged Jawar by his arms, which the king felt was a little excessive for such a small person, but he did not say a word about it. Just as they reached the doors, Jawar called out.

"Are you going to kill me?"

Before King Castilian could give his reply, the guards took him away. He did not scream, cry, or shout. The sounds of the chains rattling grew fainter, the farther away they moved from the throne room.

"I don't know," the king said, to no one.

Chapter 14:

The Dark Days

The dungeons in Raimore was one place that Jawar had never stepped foot in.

He had absolutely zero interest in seeing his people locked behind bars as if they were caged animals. His father had tried to explain the concept of criminals to him, but he just did not see it the same way he did. Yes, those who took another person's life should surely be punished for it, and stealing was sinful, but who were they to take justice into their own hands and execute someone for it? Would those acts not be just as bad as the ones committed? Jawar had, on numerous accounts, allowed a few thieves to go free in his kingdom, although he had never told his parents. They were just hungry children looking for their next meal. Maybe that made him weak and soft, but at the end of the day, Jawar knew that his morals would always remain intact.

His spirit, however, was a different story.

It had been days since the night of his arrest, and he was beginning to lose hope. There was no one in the cells adjacent to him, and he figured that had been intentional. They were trying to break him, and get him to confess to whatever treason he had committed, but it would never work. Jawar was not guilty of anything except trying to help Taviel and Raimore, and nothing more.

They had been as generous as they could be, despite his predicament. The guards brought him food twice a day; once in the morning, and once at night. It was not delicious, nor would he consider it exactly edible, but he still forced it down, not knowing how long he would remain locked up. It could be weeks, months, or even years. He doubted that last part. There was no chance that his father would go that long without having any communication with him.

Jawar wondered if King Castilian had already sent word to his father about his imprisonment. Perhaps the entire Raimore army was already on their way to break him out of jail. He tried to ask the guards for information about what was happening in the castle, but they did not speak a single word. They just slipped trays of food through the bars and went on their way.

Some nights, Jawar curled up in a far corner of the cell and used the straw as a makeshift blanket. There was a tiny window on the exterior wall, and come nightfall, the drafts made his teeth chatter. The blanket they had given him was tattered and torn, and did nothing to retain his body heat. Luckily, they had not stripped him of the garments he had been wearing, so that did give him some advantage against the cold.

But he did not know how much longer he could continue like this. As much as he wanted to remain strong, to uphold the Al Naseem name, and never bend the knee no matter what, Jawar was weak, tired, and above all, scared. Scared that he was going to die in this cell and that no one he loved would ever find out.

Right on schedule, a guard waltzed over to his cell, and this time, Jawar recognized the person standing on the other side.

"Henry?" Jawar squinted. He was the young recruit who he had met outside of Rosa's shop that one afternoon.

Looking up and down both hallways, Henry wrapped his hands around the cell bars and let out a deep sigh. "I was wondering when they were going to assign me to you."

"I didn't think I'd ever see another friendly face," Jawar winced. "Not that I'd call us friends. You probably think I'm what they say I am—a traitor."

"No, I don't," Henry replied. "You may be a prince, but you're not that good of a liar. I knew the type of person you were when I met you outside of Neo's shop. You're a good person, Jawar, one who doesn't deserve this."

"Tell that to King Castilian."

Henry chuckled, but then his face turned somber once more. "I think I'd end up in the cell next to yours if I did."

"Do you know what he plans to do with me?"

Jawar was not sure if he genuinely wanted to know. It was like what Merlin had said when they found the Dice of Destiny—our fates are already predestined; to know would only be a burden. It would just eat him alive.

"He has not said," Henry reported. "To be honest, I don't even think he knows what he's going to do with you. He seems conflicted. I don't know if it has to do with your age, or the fact that he had grown to like you during your time here, but I don't think he wants to hurt you."

"I know," Jawar sighed. "He's just doing what he needs to. That's what kings do. I'm sure my father would have done the same if the roles were reversed."

Henry squatted down and pushed the food tray into Jawar's cell. The aroma made his stomach growl. As he crawled towards it, he realized it was not the same prison food he was used to. This meal had been switched with one from the kitchen.

"I know it's not much, but it was the best I could do," Henry said. "I don't know when I'll be on this rotation again. It could be days."

Jawar grabbed handfuls of the meat pie and shoved them into his face, barely giving himself enough time to swallow between bites. He could only imagine how much of a savage he looked like, but at the moment, he did not care.

"That's if I'm still alive by then," Jawar joked.

"If I was not a new recruit, nor had a family to take care of, I would have written a letter to your father the night you were imprisoned. But I just can't take that risk. I hope you understand."

Jawar slipped his hand through the bars and held onto Henry's forearm. They stayed like that for a few beats, staring into each other's eyes. He barely knew this man, but Jawar's brief training of magic granted him the ability to sense Henry's emotions. His words were pure of heart—that much he knew.

"I'm grateful for all that you've done. Whatever happens, know that it meant the world to me."

"I should go." Henry frowned. "They'll be wondering what has taken me so long."

"Go." Jawar retracted his hand and held it close to his chest. Leaning against the bars, he did not have the strength to crawl back to his corner just yet. "Thank you for showing me kindness."

"Have hope, Prince Jawar. We have not gone to war yet. There is still time to get you out of here."

Henry disappeared down the hall, leaving Jawar to his thoughts. He did not want to tell the young guard that he was hanging on by a thread.

***

Thunder rolled in the distance, and cracks of lightning kept Jawar awake.

He had lost count of how many days had passed since his arrest. His brief visit with Henry had given him a quick burst of energy, but that too faded. Shivering, he huddled up against the bars, moving as far away from the exterior wall as he could. Rivers of water flowed from the open window, and the storm raged like a wildfire outside.

He jumped at every burst of light, and cursed himself for acting like a frightened child. He slept through storms when he was safe and sound in a plush bed with glass windows and doors, but for some reason, down in the dungeons, it was as if he were standing outside in the middle of it all.

The scent of lilacs cocooned him, and he assumed that he was finally drifting off to sleep.

Jawar? Jawar?

"Jawar? Are you awake?"

He yelped and scurried across the cell like a terrified animal. Safe without the shadows, he caught a glimpse of a silhouette and froze in place. The night guard had already come by, so who was this person standing at his cell?

"Jawar," she whispered. "You have to be quiet, please, or you'll wake the guards outside. It's me, Rosa."

"Rosa?" Jawar's voice cracked as tears came to the surface.

He had thought about her almost every day. She was one of the only rays of sunshine left in his mind. He envisioned her beautiful hair lying in waves over her shoulders, the twinkle in her eyes, and the way her lips curled into a mischievous grin whenever she gave her father a snide remark.

"Yes, it's me."

She slowly dropped to the floor and held her hand out into his cell. Timidly, he crawled on his hands and knees to the cell door until she cupped his face with her hand. The warmth of her skin made him melt. He held her hand with his own, closing his eyes for a moment, picturing himself in the blacksmith's shop, not rotting away in the dungeon.

"Is it true what they're saying about you?" Rosa pried. "Did you come to Taviel to spy on King Castilian?"

His perfect little daydream burst with those horrendous words. He fell back on his rear end, just out of reach of her touch. The last thing he wanted was to have Rosa thinking he was some kind of monster who deserved this fate.

"Would you believe me if I told you that it was all a lie?" he questioned.

"I'll believe whatever you tell me is the truth. Now answer the question. Are you a traitor to His Majesty?"

"No," he gritted through his teeth. "The only thing I am guilty of is leaving the city without his permission."

Rosa gnawed on her bottom lip as she settled in front of the cell bars, crossing her legs and fiddling with her dress. She remained quiet for a few beats before meeting his gaze once more.

"Where did you go?"

"With Merlin. We went to retrieve an artifact so he could protect it from evil sorcerers. I had left a note for King Castilian, but I now know that was a mistake. He had already suspected me of something at that point, and I just pushed him over the edge by leaving without telling him in person."

"You couldn't have known he would do this," Rosa sighed. She looked past Jawar and into the place he had called home for who knows how long. She shuddered before bringing her knees to her chest and resting her chin on top. "So you really came to Taviel for peace? So that our people could have a better life?"

Feeling his throat tighten, Jawar nodded, not wanting to cry in front of her. But it was so hard to maintain the facade. With no control, his walls came crashing down, and all he could do was let it all out. He cried for what felt like hours, but he buried his face into the crook of his elbow, not wanting the guards to hear him. He told himself it was for Rosa's sake, so she would not get caught talking with the prisoner, but he was embarrassed. From a young age, his father always taught him to never let another person see him cry.

"Tell me what I can do," she implored. "How can I fix this?"

"Rosa, there's nothing to be done. Besides, I won't let you. You are all your father has. If something were to happen to you because of me, I would never forgive myself."

This time, it was Rosa's turn to cry. It hurt Jawar's heart to see the tears stain her cheeks, and she wiped them away with the sleeve of her dress.

"I'm not going to give up on you, Jawar." She stood up, and as much as he wished to stand, and perhaps hug her through the bars, he just did not have the strength anymore. "Please hold on just a little bit longer, for me, okay? I'll come up with a plan and everything will go back to the way it was."

Yanking on the hood of her cloak, she covered her face in darkness. She lingered for a few more moments before sneaking out. Jawar used every last ounce of his strength to listen, praying that the guards had not woken up while she was in here. There was no sound of a struggle, and after a few minutes, he let his body relax. For the first time in days, or perhaps it was a few weeks by this point, Jawar fell into a deep sleep.

Chapter 15:

Please, Your Majesty

Although it had taken every last ounce of Merlin's willpower to not break King Castilian's neck with his mind, he had obeyed the King of Taviel's wishes that horrid night and stayed in his cottage.

In fact, he had not left it since. It had been almost two weeks since Jawar's arrest, and he had been surviving off of what little rations he had in his home. He had some dried fruits, nuts, wild berries, and bread that he baked every few days. It was not much, he would admit that. But he had lived in worse conditions before, and as long as he drank enough water and tea, he could survive.

Royal guards had come by every few days to check on him. He never once opened the door, and only spoke to them through the wood. They had said they were just making sure that he had not croaked in his sleep, as the people of Taviel had said he was absent from town. Merlin had been tempted to tell them why, but he assured them that he was in good health, and that they did not need to come to check on him. Still, they returned every few days, with the same questions about if he was well and letting him know that people were worried about him.

Merlin knew who it was who was worried; King Castilian. He knew he was a sorcerer, and that was no secret. He also knew that he and the little prince had some sort of connection. There was no doubt in Merlin's mind that the king feared what kind of retaliation Merlin would unleash on the kingdom should something happen to Jawar.

If he was being honest with himself, Merlin did not know. Even though there was a great distance between them, he could still sense the boy's magic. At the very least, he was alive. What frightened him was not knowing what state he was in. He prayed that King Castilian would show him an ounce of mercy. But to him, and everyone in Taviel for that matter, Jawar was a snake—a traitor—one whom they had welcomed into their kingdom and homes.

Merlin had never cared to get to know King Castilian. He assumed he was like all the other kings and royals he had met during his long life. They were all the same; pretended like they were strong-minded and superior to those they ruled, when in reality, they were just like them—scared, jealous, ignorant fools.

How could a grown man ever fear a child? What did that say about him? It made him look like a coward, that's what. Merlin had sworn an oath to himself that he would never involve himself in the political matters of the kingdom. He had come to this time to escape the wrath of the Djinn, and that was it. Excalibur was now safe within the confines of his home, along with many other precious artifacts. He had done what he had set out to do.

But now that he had met Jawar, things had become different in the blink of an eye. He had found the path he was meant to follow, without seeking the truth from the Dice, he might add. Despite his wishes to stay as far away from kingdom business as he could, Merlin could not stay silent any longer.

He had to do something or die trying.

Waving his hand over the front of his cottage, he concealed it with a simple spell, not knowing if he was going to return any time soon. He thought it was best to take all precautions, for he had no idea how far he was going to go today. He had an idea, but ideas never truly worked out in his favor. They were more like guidelines than plans.

The walk through the forest took no time at all, but that had been because his mind was bouncing all over the place. As soon as his shoes hit the cobblestones of the marketplace, familiar faces turned and pointed, and the crowds grew silent as he walked past. Wives whispered to their husbands and children tugged on their parent's hands to get their attention.

"Look, Father! Merlin is back."

Keeping his focus on the castle beyond the buzzing streets, Merlin paid them no attention, even when a few children ran up and tugged on his robes.

Successfully making his way through the marketplace, he entered through the small archway into the main courtyard. Guards were stationed at every entrance, and a few of the older soldiers immediately spotted Merlin coming and jumped into action.

"Halt, sorcerer!" a redhead shouted. "State your business here."

"I seek an audience with His Majesty King Castilian," Merlin replied. "It is of great importance, and I don't wish to doddle, so run along now and tell him that the town fool has arrived."

"King Castilian is a busy man," a bearded guard sneered. "You cannot just summon him whenever you please. We'll send word that you wish to speak to him, and when he's ready, he'll come to retrieve you from that stinking old cottage of yours."

Merlin's eyes glowed red, as these two guards were testing his patience. They took a few steps back, their hands hovering above the hilts of their swords. Their fears skyrocketed, and Merlin's dark side fed off of it. He thought he had vanquished that part of himself long ago, but the mere thought of Jawar's suffering seemed to have ignited it once more.

Just as Merlin was about to do something irrational, a young man with tousled brown hair approached. He wore the same guard's uniform as the others, but there was something different about him. It was enough to make Merlin come to his senses. His eyes returned to normal, and he forced himself to smile.

"Henry, go back to your post," the redhead said. "This does not concern you."

"I'll escort Merlin to the throne room. I have just come from there, and King Castilian is there alone. I'm sure he would not want us to dismiss this man so carelessly, given what he's capable of."

"You think I don't know he's a sorcerer?" the bearded guard barked. "I'm not scared of him."

"You should be," Henry said. "Come now, Merlin. King Castilian was wondering when you were going to come."

"I thought he might," Merlin smirked and patted the two men on the shoulders before following behind the small guard.

***

"I must admit, I underestimated you." King Castilian sat tall on his throne, desperate to look as high and mighty as he could, but Merlin could see past all that.

"In what way?" he asked.

"I thought you were going to disobey my orders and storm the castle that same night I arrested Jawar. The following night, I was convinced you would come, but again, you did not. It has been two weeks and now you've come in all your power and glory, but you seem so unbothered." The king pursed his lips, his eyes turning to slits as he tried to make sense of it all. "Why come now?"

"I stayed away for as long so that we might have a civil conversation, Your Majesty," Merlin began. "I did not want my emotions to cloud my judgment, nor yours."

'I feel nothing for the boy," King Castilian spat. "He is a traitor and deserves to be treated as such."

"Your eyes say otherwise. I can see it—the pain, the anxiety, and the complete and utter anguish that has plagued you all this time. You care, maybe too much, but you won't let the rest of them see that."

Merlin's gaze lingered on the throne room doors, where two guards stood stationed outside. The king had been clear that no one else was to enter the room besides Merlin, not even his son.

"You think you know me, sorcerer? We've barely spoken but a few words to each other since your arrival. You've made it abundantly clear that you want nothing to do with the monarchy, and I've respected that. You've remained in that shack that you call a cottage, and I've allowed it, but if you test me, I will not show you kindness."

"For a king, you do not speak with intelligence or care. You know what I am capable of, and you know what Jawar means to me. Surely, you saw it that day in the forest. We are kindred spirits, of the same kind, like he is with you. Royal blood runs through your veins, yet you treat him like a dog. Does King Umar know what you've done with his only son?"

"I do not need to share any of that information with you," King Castilian hissed. "Now, state your business or be gone. I don't have time to waste on frivolous matters such as this."

"You will free Prince Jawar and pardon him of the sentence. He will continue to live in Taviel, as the token of truce, just as you and King Umar discussed. Do this, and I will forgive your actions."

King Castilian's face turned ghostly pale. He blinked several times, as if he could not believe what he had just heard—that Merlin, a man of low blood, had the audacity to make such a demand. Never letting his gaze stray from the sorcerer, the king pushed himself from his throne and slowly descended the short steps until they stood boot to boot. Merlin was a few inches taller, and had that advantage, among other things. But Castilian had the entire kingdom at his disposal. Merlin would have to burn the city down to get to Jawar if the king did not release him.

"Have you lost your mind?" Castilian whispered.

There was a sense of shock in his tone, as if his question were one of genuine curiosity. Perhaps no one had dared to step out of line with him before, as he had never needed to establish his authority. It was just handed to him, like all the others.

"I know you're a good man," Merlin began. "Jawar bragged about you all the time. He said things were so different here in Taviel, that Raimore could learn a thing or two about the way you run your kingdom. He was so honored and so proud to be your ward. There was nothing he would not have done, had you simply asked it. So, why didn't you? When you first learned about this supposed army that King Umar was assembling, why had you not gone straight to Jawar to ask him yourself? Were you afraid of what he might say?"

"If someone were lying to you, would you confront them as plainly, or would you try to work it out yourself?" Castilian fired back. "If I had asked him and he was offended, the truce might have broken. That was a risk I was not willing to take."

"But now you are?"

"Yes," he seethed. "I have all the evidence I need."

"What evidence? Your twisted speculations? The little bits and pieces you fabricated together to make your false truth? There is nothing honest about what you have accused him of. Jawar is not a traitor, he's not conspiring against you, and he never would. Now, I'm only going to ask you this one more time. Release him, or you will regret it."

"Is that a threat, Merlin? I could have you executed on the spot for that."

"I have faced worse demons than you, Castilian. I fear no man—none as powerless as you, that is."

Merlin flexed his hand, an impulse of his dark side seeping out once more, his magic backing him should he need it.

"I might not be able to kill you, but I'm more than capable of wringing that child's neck should you step out of line. That, I can promise. I've listened to your absurd demands far longer than necessary, and I'll tell you this—Jawar can rot in that dungeon for all I care, but he will not be released. You have my word on that."

Merlin exhaled through his nostrils to regain control of his emotions. Now was not the time nor the place to show this frightened king what he could really do.

"Then you have doomed us all, and I doubt that's something you can live with for the rest of your life. King Umar will find out about this, and when he does, he will wage the grandest war, one like this kingdom has never seen. I hope you're ready for that."

With a wave of his hand, Merlin vanished in a puff of smoke, leaving the King of Taviel to ponder the sorcerer's ominous warning.

Chapter 16:

Call for the Executioner

The last few days in the prison had been surprisingly eventful.

While Jawar felt as if he were fading away to nothing, the guards were more active, antsier, and more curious about his condition. They had started to come in pairs, and that was when Jawar pieced together what had happened.

Apparently, Merlin had come a few days ago. Was it days? Jawar had lost count. He had overheard a conversation between some of the older guards, but Henry had stopped by later that same night to confirm his suspicions.

"I had been the one to escort him into the castle," Henry had admitted. "I hoped he would have been able to help, but it seems the king is not going to budge."

"Do you know what was said between the two of them?" Jawar had asked weakly.

While Henry had been gracious enough to steal him another plate from the kitchen, it was not enough to sustain him. He had begun to lose muscle mass, and what muscles remained, ached every time he moved. He did his best to remain in one spot, to preserve his energy, but at this point, there was little he could do anyway. He was just waiting for death to come for him.

"I don't know all the details," Henry had whispered, "but from what I heard, Merlin threatened the king's life. He said that he would destroy the kingdom if you were not freed."

"Then why am I still locked up?" Jawar wheezed.

"King Castilian threatened to kill you instead. That's when Merlin vanished, like a ghost. He has not been seen in the kingdom since."

Out of the few people in Taviel who knew and cared for Jawar, he hoped and prayed that Merlin would be able to set him free. He was the most powerful sorcerer in all the lands, but it seemed as if magic would not win this battle. This was a feud between Raimore and Taviel. Merlin, as sad as it was, had no business getting involved. He was not even from this time. The sand had run out on Jawar's hope for salvation.

Perhaps it had been the lack of food, or sleep, or a combination of both, but Jawar spent his hours lost in his own mind. He thought of his mother, of her sweet singing voice and the way she fluttered about the castle in beautiful gowns. She always had a way of lighting up a room, no matter who was there or what they were doing. Queen Jacia was beloved by all, and while she had a bit of a tongue and was not afraid to speak her mind, she was kind and generous, and Jawar always wanted to find a bride who his mother would be proud of. He thought of his father too, but those thoughts brought him pain and sadness. All he wanted was to make King Umar proud to call him his son, and now he was going to be the reason their kingdom fell into ruin and despair. Their lineage would be tainted forever more, and it was all because of him. He would never again share a holiday meal with his aunt, uncle, and cousins, never play in the gardens outside the castle, never listen to the birds chirping at his window, or hear Usha's laugh when he was being a little mischievous. Every last bit of happiness—the things he had taken for granted— were ripped from him in a single night.

"You are dismissed," a man ordered. Jawar was quite furious at the intrusion in his manic thoughts, but he made no effort to see who it was. "If I catch any of you down here without my consent, you will spend a week in the stocks. Do I make myself clear?"

Jawar did not hear any response, but he assumed it was not necessary. He had a clue of who was going to come around that corner, but he had no desire to speak to them. The king had done this to him—locked him up and left him for dead. Jawar was not a violent man, but for a split second, he wished he could wrap his hands around his neck and watch the life fade from his eyes.

"My heavens," the voice gasped. "I did not know what I would find when I came down here, but it was not this."

Tilting his head up, Jawar caught a glimpse of King Castilian in all his pride and glory. Or at least, that was what he had expected. Instead, what he found was a man who looked worse off than he probably did. Crouching down, he extended his hand out to touch Jawar's cheek, but he flinched out of his reach.

"Don't touch me," he growled. "You did this to me."

"I'm well aware," the king responded.

He did not sound offended, which Jawar guessed was a good thing. But it was not like there was anything worse he could do to him. Death would at least free him from his misery.

"What do you want?"

"To talk. To hear what you have to say. Your friend Merlin paid me a visit the other day, and he said you were kindred spirits. I didn't know what he had meant at the time, but I think I've pieced it together now." King Castilian paused, as if to try to find the right words to say. "Are you like him?"

Jawar managed to laugh, although pain radiated in his stomach, causing a coughing fit. When he recovered, his mouth twisted in a gruesome smile. "No one is like Merlin."

"You know what I mean. You have magic. Surely you must, for what else could he mean?"

"Even if I did, what does it matter to you?"

"Why have you not set yourself free?" he asked. "Why put yourself through all this pain and suffering if you had the power to escape?"

Jawar pondered the king's questions. He had thought about it when they first shoved him in the cell. He had wondered if his magic would be strong enough to break through the bars holding him captive. Sadly, he knew few spells that could work, and Merlin had never taught him how to harness the power within. Most of what he knew was based on instinct, something deep within himself that he never knew existed. But even if he did manage to break free, what good would that have done? The likelihood of making it far was slim, and with no real plan, Jawar bet that he would never have made it out of the main courtyard. The guards would have been told to kill him on sight and that would have been the end of it.

"I saw no point," Jawar concluded. "You already made your mind up about what I am, and what I have done."

King Castilian nodded. "A great deal has happened since you've been here, Prince Jawar—things that have brought me to this decision. Your father will arrive in Taviel any day now or it could be tomorrow for all we know. He is riding to my city as we speak and has declared war upon us. I thought that perhaps we could change the course of history, but I was wrong. There is no changing our ways. Our nations have always feuded, and it will continue unless I break the cycle."

"Break the cycle?" Jawar hesitated. "You mean—"

"You will be executed when King Umar arrives. I will make an example of you, and when you are gone, I will give him a choice; retreat and never step foot in Taviel again, or stay and fight. Either way, I'll win, and Taviel will go back to being a peaceful nation when you are gone."

Jawar did not know what the king wanted him to say. Perhaps he wanted him to put up a fight, confess, or both. He let out a deep sigh, his eyes drifting shut for a moment. It took every fiber of his being to stay awake. He squinted, and that was when he realized that the king was holding something in his hands.

"What's that?" Jawar asked.

"The letters from your father," he stated. "I thought you might like to read them before he comes so you can see for yourself why I have left you to rot in this cell."

With that, King Castilian shoved the papers through the cell and retreated without another word. Jawar stared at the pile of parchment for a few moments, watching the dirt and rainwater stain the edges. Groaning, he reached forward to gather them up. He had no idea that the king and his father were in constant communication with each other. Starting from the one dated the farthest back, Jawar read out loud.

"King Castilian, it has come to my attention that you do not wish to stay true to your word about our truce. If this is true, send my son home in peace and we will work this out together. There is no need to harm Jawar. Signed, King Umar."

Jawar's throat bobbed. Not wanting to stop and wallow in the words, he flipped to the next letter.

"King Castilian, if you continue to threaten my only heir and son, I will not hesitate to take drastic measures to retrieve him. There is still time to uphold the peace between our two nations, but I'm willing and prepared to go to war if we must. Signed, King Umar."

Frustrated, he flipped to the most recent one, unable to get through the dozen sitting in his lap.

"King Castilian, I know you have imprisoned my son and I will sit idle no longer. We are coming; me, my army, and my brother, and we will lay waste to Taviel until only you and your children remain. Then, I will pluck them from the earth, and leave you to rot. I hope for your sake that Jawar is still alive. Signed, King Umar."

Jawar blinked, shocked by the words he just read. That did not sound like his father. None of them did. He was an advocate for peace—he had been for Jawar's entire life. That was why coming to Taviel had been so important to him; even though he was going to miss watching his son grow up and become a young man, in the end, he knew it would be worth it.

Most of the letters had fallen off his lap, but the last one remained. He ran his fingers over the seal. It was

King Umar's signature seal. That much was for certain. But how could he do this? He must have known that sending these threats—these atrocious letters—would have repercussions for Jawar's life. Did he no longer care? Did he think King Castilian did not have it in him to hurt a 13-year-old prince?

Looking at the letter once more, Jawar's heart skipped a beat.

These correspondences may have had the king's seal, but they were not written by the king's hand. He knew King Umar's handwriting well, as he had been the one who helped Jawar when he was little. The tutors had been frustrated because Jawar could never hold the quill right. It was why his and his father's handwriting looked so similar.

Someone forged these letters. That was the only explanation. Jawar fumbled in his cell to try to get one of the guard's attention, but it was of no use. King Castilian had dismissed them all, and he had no idea when or if they were coming back.

Sobbing, his legs kicked out from underneath him as he pressed his back against the cell bars. He reached out for the final letter again and read it three more times, hoping that something would jump out at him.

My brother.

It was written differently, angrier. The tip of the quill had scratched at the back of the parchment, leaving an indentation. Jawar squeezed his eyes shut, trying to make the pieces in his head fit together.

My brother.

"Hakim!" he gasped.

It had been his uncle the whole time. He had been the one writing these threats, not King Umar. But why? Jawar, clenching the pile of lies in his hands, clenched his jaw so tightly that his ears popped. He feared he would never live long enough to find out.

Chapter 17:

Declaration of War

It had been the dead of night when King Umar's peaceful sleep was interrupted by an eerie sound.

At first, he had figured that it was just a dream, a nightmare really, for the only time he had ever heard those horns was during times of war. Umar had suffered from the same recurring nightmare in the past. There were just some things that he could never force himself to forget. And while he slept, his mind was more vulnerable, and it could play tricks on him, if he was not careful.

This was another one of those times. As long as he acknowledged that this was all in his head, that he was safe and sound in his bed, with his wife next to him, the dream would pass.

But it did not.

The war horns continued to blow louder and louder.

"Umar, what is that awful noise?" Jacia whined into her pillow, her eyes still shut.

She was barely awake, but her voice grounded Umar. He realized that it was not just inside of his head, for she could hear it too. That was not a good sign. That meant that it was not just a dream.

"I don't know, darling, but I'll go find out and be back before you know it."

Umar, getting on in his years, struggled to sit upright. Blinking several times, he ran his hands over his face, trying to wake himself up more. The door burst open, crashing against the wall, and Jacia screamed, scrambling to grab hold of her husband. He nearly jumped out of his own skin, and somehow managed to fall off the bed, hitting his head against the end table as he did so. He cursed, rubbing his scalp tenderly, furious that anyone in the kingdom would dare enter their private bedchambers in such a manner.

"Brother, it's me." Hakim hauled Umar to his feet, giving him a good slap on the cheek to orient himself. "Something terrible has happened."

"What is it?" Umar grunted. He glanced at his wife, who had pulled the bed sheets up to her throat, as she was wearing something no brother-in-law should ever see.

"Your worst nightmare has become a reality!" Hakim rushed. "I'm afraid Prince Jawar has been imprisoned in Taviel."

"What?" Jacia gasped. "What are you talking about?"

"I just received this letter now, from King Castilian himself. It explains everything. Go on, read it yourself."

He thrust it into King Umar's trembling hands. He had only read the first sentence when Jacia demanded that he read it for all of them to hear.

"King Umar," he cleared his throat. "This has been the final straw between our two nations. Raimore and Taviel will never know peace. I have found Prince Jawar guilty of treason against myself and the crown and have since placed him in prison for said crimes. I caught him conspiring against me, following an order no doubt that came from you. When I discovered that this token of truce was all a lie, I did what was necessary for my country and kingdom. If you try to come for him, you will force my hand. Leave him a prisoner of war, and I will seek no further action against you. Signed, King Castilian of Taviel."

The crippling silence could have swallowed the room whole. Umar stood frozen like a statue, waiting for either his wife or brother to speak first. Jacia let out a bone-chilling sob and Umar rushed to her bedside to comfort her as best as he could.

"I cannot believe this has happened!" she wailed. "My only son, my baby boy, locked up in a dungeon like some kind of criminal. This is madness. Umar, tell me this is just a terrible nightmare, please!"

"Hush, my darling Jacia. You'll only stress yourself out more. You cannot break now, not when Jawar needs us most."

He grabbed her hands and squeezed them as tightly as he could, hoping that it would pull her back to this hellish reality. Tears streamed down her face, and her eyes were so swollen that he wondered how they were still open. She placed her forehead against his and continued to cry.

"What are we going to do, Umar? He threatened to kill our son. He's just a boy, he is not fit for war."

"He's old enough," Hakim interjected.

"Stay out of this, brother, or so help me!" Umar pointed his finger and shouted, his hands shaking out of control. "You are as much to blame as any of us. You were the one who suggested Jawar go to Taviel in the first place, not me. You and King Castilian negotiated the terms on my behalf. If this is anyone's fault, it's yours."

"I have done nothing but stand by your side in all these weeks and months that Jawar has been gone," Hakim defended. "I have been the one assembling the troops in case something like this happened, I have been promoting generals and sending out conscriptions to hire new recruits. The only reason you have an army strong enough to go against Taviel is because of me."

"We never wanted to go to war!" Umar screamed. "That was the whole point of sending Jawar away! It was a sign of peace! Can't you see that?"

"Whatever has happened, we can fix it. Surely King Castilian will see reason. He must. This is all just talk, these letters, you don't actually think he would execute your son, do you? We are more civilized than our ancestors."

"If he does, Jawar's blood is on your hands," Jacia whimpered. "I never should have let him go. He could be sleeping down the hall in his bed right now, not curled up and frightened in some filthy cell."

"Alright, let's all just calm down," Umar huffed. "Arguing with each other is not going to get our son back. We need to think rationally, and someone needs to stop blowing those forsaken horns!"

Hakim dismissed himself momentarily, allowing Jacia and Umar time to cool off. They sat in silence for a few minutes, staring at the wall, their hands just barely touching. Umar did not know what to think, or do, for that matter. If he lost Jawar, Jacia would never forgive him. Their marriage and lives would be over.

"I want you to promise me something," she said finally. Umar turned his head to look at her, and her face was expressionless—void of all emotion. Even the tears had dried on her cheeks, and her eyes were dark and empty. "Get Jawar back. I don't care what you have to do, just do it. Kill King, Castilian for all I care. Burn their cities to the ground. Bring Jawar home so we can be done with all of this."

"I will," Umar vowed.

He did not recognize his wife's voice. He hoped that she was still inside, buried beneath the heartache and sorrow. Not that he blamed her for what she was feeling, as he was too, but it still shocked him to his very core. He was afraid to even reach out to touch her shoulder, for he did not know what she would do.

Hakim returned less than half an hour later and this time, he was wearing his war armor, and he had some of the staff carry in Umar's. It had been a long time since he had seen it, and now he was expected to put it on and walk straight into battle. They laid it out meticulously in the sitting room adjacent to their sleeping quarters, down to the belt.

"I never thought I would have to wear this again," Umar admitted.

Hakim gave his brother a somber look as he snapped his fingers for the servants to begin dressing the king. They worked in silence, and before he knew it, he was head to toe in nothing but metal. He was a bit embarrassed to admit that it was a little tight on him now, as he had been a young man when he wore it last. Jawar had not even been born at that time. Umar desperately wanted to forge a new world for his son, one where he would never have to fight someone just because they lived in a different country and had different views.

He was foolish to think that King Castilian wanted the same for Prince Darrow. If only he had realized it sooner.

Hakim cleared his throat. "I can't imagine what you must be feeling right now. If this were my child, I would do the unthinkable to make sure he was safe. I want you to know that I'm going to fight for Jawar until my dying breath, as if he were my son. He is my flesh and blood, as he is yours. We're going to do this together, as a family."

"Thank you, brother," Umar nodded. "I feel as though I'm drowning in a sea of uncertainty. Here I have been parading around the castle, not even seeing the truth as it was right in front of me, but you've known all along, haven't you? That this truce was never going to work out the way we planned."

Hakim's shoulders dropped, and for a few beats, he could not stand to hold his brother's mighty gaze. "I had hoped that it would. I wanted a better life for my children too, Umar. But the truth is, no amount of words and wishes can change generations of conflict and bloodshed. While I had hope, I also had to be realistic. That's why I had been preparing, just in case."

Umar was tempted to bid his wife farewell, but he did not want to disturb her—not while she was in a state of shock. The last thing she needed was to see him dressed for battle. He wondered if he was ever going to be able to hold his beautiful wife in his arms again. He also wondered if he was going to return home at all. He was not as tough as he had been in his youth, and age had caught up with him, as it had with Hakim. Perhaps that would be his only advantage, that King Castilian would find fighting difficult as well. That fire had long burned out in Umar's heart.

"Tierra," Umar sighed. She looked on the edge of tears herself, and the king had no doubt in his mind that she had caught wind of Jawar's current situation. She had helped to raise him, and likely saw him as a second son. "I need you to take care of my wife while I'm gone. Make sure she eats, gets out of bed at least once a day, preferably goes outside for at least half an hour, and that she bathes—even if you have to drag a wet cloth across her skin while she lays in bed."

"Of course, Your Majesty." Tierra blinked. "I will do anything and everything to make sure she is comfortable."

"There's a chance I might not come back," he lowered his voice in case Jacia could hear them. "Jawar, too. She will be all that is holding Raimore up, and I need her to be strong for our kingdom."

"We will protect her," Tierra promised. "Usha, too."

"Good. Thank you, for all that you two have done for my family. The queen and I... Well, we were busy during Jawar's childhood, and I realize now that we did not spend as much time with him as we should have. But you two were always there. I'm grateful he had such wonderful people watching out for him."

Tierra's bottom lip trembled and out of nowhere, she wrapped her arms around Umar's neck and hugged him with all her might. Normally, he would have protested and dismissed her for being so wildly inappropriate, but right now, he did not care in the slightest. He hugged her back, allowing himself a few final moments of normalcy before he walked out of the castle, for what he hoped would not be the last time.

"Are you ready, Umar?" Hakim asked as they strode toward the main entrance.

"No. But what choice do I have?"

Hakim's lip curled into an unsettling smile. Umar had no idea why, but he felt as if he were enjoying all the chaos. "That's the spirit."

Chapter 18:

I'm Coming For You,

Merlin

The last time that Hakim had traveled this close to Raimore and Taviel's borders, it had been under entirely different circumstances.

While it had only been a few short months ago, looking back on it now, it felt like a whole lifetime. Jawar was just a naive little boy who was excited to be moving to a new country. He had so much hope in his eyes—so much wonder and goodness. Hakim could barely stand to witness it. If only his nephew knew the truth, the whole truth, perhaps his life could have been spared.

There were few things that Hakim wanted in this world, and one of those things was in Taviel. But Jawar was not his flesh and blood. He could die in that cell, for all he cared. No, what he wanted was far greater than life itself. And there was nothing that was going to get in his way. He was willing to cut down his own brother if it came to that. He was not about to let months of months of meticulous planning, deceit, and betrayal all go to waste over the life of one person, who, by the sounds of the real letters he had received from King Castilian, had been locked up for quite some time now. The only difference was that he was willing to strike a bargain with King Umar, believing that peace was still obtainable if they stopped the madness before it got out of hand.

Hakim had made sure that those letters never reached his brother's hands. If they had, then the chances of him marching across the countryside to storm their enemy's castle would be slim to none.

"What do you think, Hakim?" Umar invaded his brother's vile thoughts. He glanced at his older brother, raising his eyebrows, signaling that he had unfortunately not been listening to the conversation.

"Sorry, I didn't hear that last part," he admitted.

"I said what do you think about setting up camp here for the night?" Umar repeated. "We are less than a few hours away from Taviel's border. I don't think they would be foolish enough to cross into Raimore, not if they know we are coming with 10 thousand men. If we get some rest and get up at dawn, we can make it to the capital city by midday tomorrow."

"Perhaps even sooner," Hakim agreed. "I do recall the journey to the royal city was quick, once we had crossed the bridge."

"Sure, but it was just three carriages then. Half of our soldiers aren't even on horseback. It'll take more time than that."

"Whatever you want, is what we'll do," Hakim snapped. "Just make a decision so we can get on with it."

Umar glared at his younger brother for a few beats, and for a moment, Hakim feared that he had crossed a line. Even if they were on the very cusp of war, he was still expected to obey His Majesty as if they were back in the castle. Little did Umar know that they were very far from home indeed, and that Hakim had other plans.

"Raja," Umar addressed one of their highest-ranking generals. "Send some of your men ahead and let them know that we are camping here for the night. Once we are settled, I want at least one hundred men scouting the area to make sure that we are not ambushed. Guard rotations will be every hour. Everyone should already know their duties, but if anyone looks lost, give them something to do. This is war, general, I want things done and I want them done fast."

"Yes, Your Majesty." Raja flicked the reins of his horse and rode off ahead, along with half a dozen soldiers.

Umar exhaled a deep sigh before turning to his younger brother. "Satisfied?" he seethed.

"Very. You're starting to sound more like my brother and not whatever that peace-pushing mush you had become."

"Careful," Umar warned. "You may be my brother, but I'll still throw you into the stocks for insubordination."

Hakim could not help but laugh at his brother's feeble attempts to threaten him. "Take a look around, Umar. We're nowhere near any form of civilization. You may be King of Raimore, but right now, you're just like the rest of us—a soldier marching to his death. Besides, there may not be anything to go back to once we're through here. Maybe I'll end up as the new king."

The look on Umar's face was more satisfying than anything that Hakim had seen in his entire life. "Set up your tent next to mine," he growled. "I want to keep my eye on you."

"Yes, Your Majesty." Hakim smiled.

Hakim dismounted from his horse and handed the reins to one of the young boys walking on foot. "Do as the king said. Set up the tent and let me know when it's finished. I have work to do and I need a private space to do it."

"Yes, Your Grace. Right away."

***

Hakim settled into his tent within an hour.

They had little to travel with across the countryside, but being of royal status did have some perks. It meant that he did not have to sleep beneath the stars like an animal, and could actually get some decent rest on a sleeping mat and pillow. He was also granted a small sitting table for eating and working at, as well as other luxuries like oil lamps and good meals with the snap of his fingers.

Whipping open the flap of his tent, he whistled at the young soldier who had assembled his tent. "You! I need you to locate three of my generals and let them know I'm requesting their presence immediately."

The young man nodded, knowing that he had no other choice. "Their names, Your Grace?"

"Roman, Amaro, and Eddard. Tell me you can tell the difference between a general's insignia and a captain's."

"Of course. We learned it in training camp. I could draw them for you, if you don't believe me."

"No," Hakim sighed, waving him off like he was a flea. "Just do as I ask and make it quick."

Just as the sun was beginning to set, Hakim's most trusted advisors arrived at his tent. Roman, the bravest of the bunch, stuck his head in without even announcing his presence. "You called, Your Grace?"

Hakim's heart skipped a beat as he scrambled to cover his journals with a loose piece of parchment. For all he knew, it could have been his brother, and his entire plan would have been spoiled, just like that.

"You fool," Hakim growled. "I thought you were Umar."

"Apologies," Amaro snickered. "You did summon us. Surely you knew we would come eventually?"

"Yes, but permission to enter my tent is required," he gritted through his teeth. "Where is the soldier who brought you here?"

"Standing outside." Eddard pointed his thumb over his shoulder nonchalantly. "Shall I tell him to scram?"

"Politely, and without drawing unwanted attention to yourself," Hakim ordered.

Eddard disappeared for less than a minute before he was back inside the confines of his master's tent.

"That was quick," Roman said.

"I just told him that if he didn't leave within five seconds, that I would assign him to a less than ideal duty. He conveniently remembered that he had not been served his dinner portion yet and that he would be gone for some time."

"Excellent." Hakim grinned. "Now, let's get done to business before Umar returns from his council meeting with Raja and the other generals."

"That reminds me. Won't they be wondering where we've gone?" Roman perched himself on the edge of Hakim's table, nibbling at some of the dried fruit and nuts as if they belonged to him. "We're generals, are we not? It is not required for us to be there?"

"I'll make up an excuse. Don't worry about that. We have more pressing matters to focus on."

"Your nephew?" Amaro chuckled. "Oh wait, you don't care what happens to him."

"Lower your voice or someone might hear you," Hakim growled. "You want this as much as I do, and I need your word that you're going to do exactly as I say."

"We've already pledged our loyalty to you," Roman interjected, "well before that brat ever stepped foot in Taviel."

"Then you know what needs to be done."

"Secure the sorcerer before everything unravels into chaos, we know." Roman sighed and leaned back onto his hands before crossing one leg over his knee. "What's changed?"

"A lot, unfortunately." Hakim sneered. "I was not able to tell you earlier, but the last letter that came from King Castilian proved more valuable than all the others. As it turns out, my darling nephew is rather close with our target. In fact, the king mentioned that he had tried to threaten him to have Jawar released."

"So?" Eddard asked.

"It means if King Castilian plans to make a scene with Jawar's execution, chances are that Merlin will be there. He'll try to stop it, so kidnapping him will be much more difficult with thousands of Raimore and Taviel soldiers standing there watching."

The three generals went quiet, piecing together Hakim's revelation. Their plans to sneak off in the midst of battle to track down the sorcerer were not going to work. They needed to make a few last-minute changes, and that made Hakim antsy. He had put much effort into making sure that Umar and his army kept the rest of the kingdom preoccupied while he slipped in to get his real prize.

Merlin.

The legendary sorcerer he had heard so many grand tales about and the one who had countless magical artifacts—things that Hakim could use to his advantage. And with Excalibur to top it all off, he would have everything he ever wanted. Endless power and a ruined kingdom to rebuild would be his, and when it rose from the ashes, it would not be because of some frivolous peace treaty. No, it would be because of blood, sweat, and sacrifices.

He just hoped that Umar and Jawar would be long dead before he claimed his place in Raimore. The only issue would be the lovely Queen Jacia. Getting rid of her would be no easy task, as Tierra had made it clear that they were not going to leave her unattended. Hopefully, Merlin would be able to concoct some untraceable magic potion that he could slip into her tea, or maybe even just manipulate her mind to the point that she went mad. Hakim did not care to work out the details just yet.

First, he had to get the sorcerer. Then, everything would fall into place.

"What are we going to do about it? The only solution is to—"

"Get in and get out before dawn," Roman revealed. "But I thought you said that Umar is going to be keeping a watchful eye on you."

"He is, which is why we leave now. I hope you brought your things, because it's now or never, and believe me, I'm not about to let this chance slip away."

Ronald, Amaro, and Eddard all saluted in unison. Hakim was grateful that he could count on their loyalty. He never would have been able to do anything like this without them. He had promised that they would be able to have their pick of the artifacts once Hakim got what he wanted. They could fight over the scraps all they wanted. As long as they remembered who was to be their future king, that was all that mattered.

And Hakim would be king. With Merlin's help, it would be guaranteed.

A part of him feared that his wife and children would never understand the sacrifices he had to make to give them the life they deserved. He was willing to slaughter his own flesh and blood to rise through the ranks, and he knew how much his sons loved their cousin. If they ever found out that he had been the one to set him up since the very beginning, they could very well turn their backs on him. Treading carefully was the only way that this plan would work.

"We're ready if you are," Ronald spoke for the group. "Like you said, it's now or never."

Retrieving a letter from his breast pocket, he placed it on the desk for Umar to find. He had read it so many times over the last few weeks that he had memorized it word for word.

Umar—I've taken some of your best generals to scout a possible ambush on the south side of the forest. If I don't come back, tell my wife and children that I love them and that I died with honor. Do not send anyone after me. This is something I have to do for myself, for you, and for Jawar. Like you said, I'm partly to blame for all that has happened. Let me fix this. Let me build us a new world—one we always dreamed of.

The last sentence was the most important. He did plan to build a new world, one where magic would reign over them all, and Hakim would be standing right behind, pulling the strings.

Chapter 19:

The Great Escape

After his unexpected visit from King Castilian, Jawar, for the first time in weeks, held a flicker of hope.

It had nothing to do with what the king had said. He made it abundantly clear that he was to be used as an example of what happened to those who crossed him. No, Jawar had hope because he knew that Castilian was wrong about Raimore and wrong about the fact that they were the first to assemble an army. He was also wrong about the reason that King Umar had sent Jawar to Taviel in the first place. He was wrong about everything.

His father had not been the cruel man behind those threatening letters. His uncle had been. Why? Jawar had still not figured out that part yet, but he had a few theories—ones that were all too familiar over the course of history. The typical younger brother, resentful that he had to live in the shadows of his older brother and craving power that would never truly belong to them.

Jawar had heard it over and over during his history lessons with the tutors, both Master Tal and the ones back home. Even Merlin, a sorcerer from hundreds of years past, had said the same thing. History has a way of repeating itself, and now, it was happening before the prince's very eyes.

He did not know if it was his sense of purpose that gave him the strength to pace around the cell day and night. It had been so long, that his muscles continued to burn and ache from lack of use, but he gritted his teeth and pushed past it all. As long as he focused on the task at hand, that was all that mattered. However, getting the attention of the guards had proven to be more difficult than he had anticipated.

They were rough and ruthless, shaking the bars of the cell and shouting that his death day was on the horizon. Jawar had tried to plead with them, holding up the remnants of the letters and saying that none of them had come from his father's hand. But they were blinded, like all the rest—blinded by the lust for blood and vengeance. While his odds were not good, Jawar was not going to go down without a fight. This was not how his journey would end.

"What's that?" a man's voice asked.

Jawar, having been muttering to himself as he walked back and forth in the small space, looked up to find Henry, alone. His head was tilted to the side as he looked the little prince up and down, and he could have sworn that there was a hint of a smile tugging at the corners of his mouth.

"You look different than the last time I saw you."

"I've had a bit of a revelation," Jawar stated. "Everything King Castilian believes is a lie."

"Yes, we've been over that, probably a dozen times. What's different now that you've got a spring in your step?"

"I have proof!" Jawar grabbed the crinkled parchment and practically shoved it in Henry's face through the metal that was keeping him captive. "He claims that these are from my father. Yes, they have his official seal, but it's not his handwriting. I should know, as he was the one who taught me. I would recognize it anywhere."

Henry's eyebrows pinched together as he tried to make sense of what Jawar was insinuating. "You mean to tell me that they were forged? That sounds awfully convenient, Jawar, a little too much if you ask me."

"Why would I lie now?" Jawar crossed his arms over his chest.

"Because you're about to be executed?" Henry questioned.

Jawar's shoulders dropped, feeling his sense of hope slipping away as if it were never there in the first place. "Do you not believe me? Do you think I am what they all say?"

Henry reached out and placed a hand on the bar separating the two of them. Jawar could almost see himself in the glossy surface of his eyes. He looked rough. He did not even look at all like himself anymore.

"It means nothing if I believe you or not, which I do, by the way. I don't know why, but I can just tell. Yet I'm just a single guard who has no real say in what happens in the kingdom. You have to convince King Castilian, with your dying breath if necessary. Do you understand me? Don't give up."

With that, the guard continued his nightly rotation, not wanting to linger too long in the lowest part of the dungeons. The place is especially reserved for the criminals accused of treason. While Jawar had been the only one to grace its presence in the last few weeks, he knew that there had to be others before him. Every one of these cells was occupied at some point. The blood stains were proof of that.

What Jawar needed most was time—time to get a plan together so he could figure out a way to prove that Hakim was behind all this, not King Umar. He did not know what that would mean for his uncle. Would he find himself on the other end of the executioner's blade, or would King Castilian leave it up to his father? Either way, it was something that Jawar would not have to deal with. As long as he did not let his mind wander, he could keep his wits about himself.

His head felt like it might explode from how much he had tried to come up with a plan to get out of the dungeons, when all of a sudden, there was a shuffling sound outside of his prison window. Jawar stopped, tilting his head up to the ceiling to focus on the sounds. Boots crunched underneath the pebbles, squelching in the mud, as it had just recently rained.

Whoever it was, did not speak a word, but something fell inside of Jawar's cell, making a dull clanging noise when it hit the floor. Glancing over his shoulder to make sure that no guards had been walking by at the time, Jawar quickly retrieved the mysterious item and removed the twine and cloth that concealed the contents.

It was a brass key with a rolled piece of parchment attached. Could it be? Jawar nearly slammed his body against the cell door to examine the keyhole. It looked completely different from the shape of the key in his hands. How was this supposed to help?

Mumbling under his breath, he unraveled the note to find a few scribbles by a familiar hand.

"I have charmed this key to be able to unlock any door that should cross your path. Get out and run as fast as your feet can carry you. Meet me where it all began, M."

"Thank you, Merlin," Jawar's voice cracked.

He squeezed his eyes shut, feeling his throat tighten up for a few seconds, but he pushed past the tears, telling himself that he could cry when this was all over. Right now, he just needed to follow his mentor's advice—get out and run.

The hardest part had been waiting for the next guard's rotation to go by. He continued to pace as normally as he could, despite the fact that he now possessed a way to get out. Right on schedule, a single guard came down the hall to check in on him. He had a red beard and was one of the regular guards assigned to his watch. He never said a single word, and unlike some of the younger guards, did not taunt or poke at Jawar. He merely looked to make sure that he was still locked up and was then on his way.

Perfect. That was all he needed—a big gap of time where he would be undisturbed.

Holding his breath, Jawar fiddled with the massive key until it was flush with the hole to his cell. Before his very eyes, the eye glowed a bright yellow and it morphed and molded itself to fit inside the cell lock. With a quick twist, there was an audible click. Jawar did not think he had heard a more beautiful sound in all his life.

Clenching his jaw tight, he pushed open the cell door as quietly as he could. It creaked slightly, as the hinges were rusted from lack of use. Not once had a single guard dared to open it, and neither had the king. Why would he, when it was suspected that he was a sorcerer just like Merlin. For all he knew, that could have been part of Jawar's master plan. Sit and wait for the king to come to him, so he could make a mockery of his attempts to keep him behind bars.

Well, his nightmares had become real. It may not have been his magic that set him free, but it had been magic, nonetheless.

Stepping out into the hallway, Jawar's knees threatened to buckle underneath him, but he ignored the weariness as best as he could. He used the walls for assistance, propping himself up as he hobbled along, hoping that he would use the least amount of energy that way. He tried to remember the route by which they had brought him here, but it had been so long ago, and his mind was still foggy from all the days he spent daydreaming his life away.

"You!"

Jawar whirled around to find two guards descending upon him like hell hounds. He barely had any time to think, much less do anything. The second they touched his arms, it was as if he burst into flames. A blast erupted from the center of his chest, sending the two guards flying. They connected with the far wall before collapsing to the ground in an unnatural way.

He knelt by their sides, placing his hand on their chests, praying that he had not just killed them by accident. Although their breaths were shallow, they were still alive, and that was good enough.

It was a task all in itself climbing the stairs to reach the top level of the dungeon where the rest of the prisoners were held. Some of them begged Jawar to give them the key to set them free. As much as he wished to help, knowing that they were suffering just as he was downstairs, he did not have the time to stop. He had to think about himself, even if it went against everything that he believed in.

"I'm so sorry," he said to the family of three, huddled in the cell closest to him.

It was a mother with her two children, and he could only imagine why they had been imprisoned. By the looks of their clothes and sunken faces, he figured that stealing food had to be the reason. Jawar promised himself that he would return to free them all. He just needed a real plan—not a sorcerer's magic key.

"It's fine," the mother whispered. "Save yourself."

Her words said one thing, but her eyes said another. Maybe this would be a good thing, he thought. A distraction. Fetching the key from his trouser pocket, he stepped in front of her cell and pressed the key against the lock. Once again, it morphed into the required shape, and the woman gasped, likely having never seen magic in action before.

When it was the perfect fit, Jawar twisted the lock and pushed the cell open, offering the frightened woman a hand.

"You're a magic wielder?" she asked timidly, her children clutching her legs as she stepped out.

"I am," Jawar said proudly. "Now, use this key to set everyone else you can free. The guards will be by any second, so you don't have much time. Whatever you do, don't get caught. Do you understand me?"

"Yes, but what about the key? Surely it's too valuable for you to give away."

Jawar looked at the piece of brass sitting in the palm of her hand. "It fulfilled its purpose."

Chapter 20:

The Enchanted Cottage

Jawar was grateful for the fact that the dungeons were close to the same exit that he had used to sneak off to Merlin's cottage in the middle of the night.

The tunnel underneath the castle was empty, and not even a single torch was lit. What was even better, was the fact that he had lost a few pounds while locked up, so it was easy to slip between the two gates held together by a single chain.

His prison break felt too easy. He feared that at any moment, King Castilian would emerge from the shadows and laugh at his feeble attempts to get away, as if this were all just a wicked game meant to entertain them before he was hauled away to be executed. He tried his best to not let those dark thoughts seep into his mind because if he allowed them to linger too long, he might slip up and then it would have all been for nothing.

Hobbling his way into the marketplace, he felt as if he was in a haunted graveyard. There were no torches, and no civilians taking midnight strolls under the moonlight. Sticking close to the shadows, he spotted a few of the guards stationed at the entrance to the castle courtyard, and there were several others walking about.

Taviel was on high alert. Any minute now, he suspected that the bells would chime, signaling that he had escaped. But until then, he had to be quick and quiet. Stealth would be his saving grace, as much as he was tempted to blast them all with his magic again. He was not sure if it would work a second time, if he were being honest. His magic seemed to feed off of his fear or his desperation, but that was not reliable.

Never letting his gaze wander from the guards closest to the road he was heading for, Jawar practically became one with the stone wall. He thought about climbing it and walking across the top, but with his luck, someone might see, and then he would be trapped. That idea quickly fell through.

With his heart hammering in his chest, and his thighs burning with every step, Jawar successfully slipped past the two guards. He had made it into the marketplace unseen. Now, all he had to do was race across town and head for Merlin's cottage in the depths of the forest. It all sounded easier said than done.

He had barely made it down the first street in the marketplace when the bells started to ring. So, they had discovered his escape. He prayed that the other prisoners would keep them occupied long enough so that he could put more distance between himself and the castle. But that was wishful thinking. At the end of the day, they did not care to contain a mother stealing a loaf of bread, or a man who had been unable to pay his taxes. They were after Jawar—the real prize—the kingdom's most wanted traitor.

Dozens of hooves pounded against the cobblestone street. It only made Jawar run faster.

"Find him!" a man shouted into the night. "Before he reaches the forest!"

Passing by the blacksmith's shop, he contemplated hiding inside. Any one of the shops in this district would be a viable place to hold up until the coast was clear, but there was something about this place that felt like home. He stared at his reflection in the glass for a moment, recalling the last time he had seen Rosa with her beautiful scarf tying her hair back as she worked and listening to her and Neo banter back and forth as they forged the weapons that the guards were now trying to use against him.

As much as he wanted to see their faces, hug them, and perhaps indulge himself in Neo's famous stew, he knew that it was a bad decision to get them involved. The last thing he wanted was to have them accused of aiding a traitor. Just as he was about to push on, a guard approached from behind, and grabbed him by the back of his tunic.

Jawar yelped, throwing his fist to try to knock the guard off of his horse. But he dodged his weak attacks and hoisted Jawar up onto the steed.

"Is that any way to treat a friend?" Henry sneered, but there was a hint of playfulness in his voice.

"Henry." Jawar sighed with relief.

Realizing he was not in any immediate danger, he readjusted himself on the horse and let his legs relax. They burned like a thousand fires, but he was not out of the gate just yet. There was still time for him to be captured. Maybe he had misjudged his friendship with Henry, and he planned to bring him back to the castle. He would not hold it against him. He would probably be declared a war hero and given a promotion in the army.

But instead of turning back and going the way he had come, Henry guided his horse toward the edge of the forest.

"Why are you helping me?" Jawar whispered.

"Like I said before, I know you're a good man. But I can only bring you so far. I'll drop you off where the marketplace ends, and then you will be on your own. I'll do what I can to steer them away, but I make no promises. This last part is going to be the toughest, but I have that faith you'll make it there in time."

"Make it where?"

"Where else," Henry mused. "Merlin's cottage. Who do you think helped him to bring you the key?"

So, this was all part of their plan. Maybe it was going to work after all. He had people on the outside who did care if he lived or died.

Reaching their destination, Jawar slipped off of the horse with ease. Or rather, he would have, if he had not been locked up for weeks and severely malnourished. His legs crumbled beneath him, and his face planted on the cobblestone street. He could have sworn that he heard a crack as his nose broke his fall, and blood gushed from his nostrils. Henry circled around him a few times, waiting for him to get to his feet.

"Can you walk?"

Groaning, he wiped the blood on the back of his sleeve and pushed himself up. He let out a few deep sighs, tilting his face to the moonlight to harness some of its energy. "Even if I couldn't, I'd crawl my way there."

"That's the spirit," Henry smirked. "Now go. They'll be riding up and down this border trying to cut you off. Make haste, but do so quietly. Whatever you do, don't come back, no matter what."

"Thank you again, for saving my life." Jawar placed his hand over his heart. It was to signify his eternal gratitude. "If I live through this horrific nightmare, I shall see to it that you are rewarded."

"I didn't do this because you're a prince and I thought I might get something out of it," Henry said, as he flicked his horse's reins. "You're special, Jawar. I know you will do great things."

With that, Henry took off into the night, the sounds of the hooves against the cobblestone echoing in the distance. Jawar did not give himself a moment of rest. He took off into the forest, not slowing down for the branches overhead, even as they slashed him in the face. The little cuts stung, but whatever King Castilian had in store for him back at the castle would be far worse than this.

Zigzagging down the familiar path, Jawar misjudged the height of an overgrown root and nearly twisted his ankle. He fell among the rocks and branches, his head narrowly colliding with a boulder the size of his torso. His body screamed to stop, for every muscle in his body ached like never before. But he was so close. He could see the tiny orange light just up ahead.

Merlin's cottage.

It was less than a hundred paces away. "Come on, Jawar," he gritted through his teeth. "You're almost there."

"I see him!"

The voice belonged to someone who did not want to save the little prince from his waking nightmare. Looking over his shoulder, he spotted a few guards on horseback, and feared that he had run out of time. Crying in pain, he pushed himself back up and raced as fast as his feet could carry him. They were closing the gap, but Jawar did not dare to look back. If he did, he might fall again, and then surely it would be over.

Skipping the three steps of Merlin's porch, he burst through the doors and collapsed onto the floor.

Merlin leaped out of his seat and raised his arms above his head. He spoke an incantation—one that Jawar did not recognize. A golden light burst from his fingertips and the door slammed shut.

"It's no use," Jawar wheezed. "They're already here."

Merlin dropped to his knees and turned Jawar onto his back to assess the damage. Jawar was in rough shape, not just from his time spent in the cell, but from his travels through the marketplace and forest. His nose was most definitely broken, and he did not think that his legs would ever recover again.

"They cannot see us anymore," Merlin explained. "I cast a protection spell around the cottage, making it invisible. They might know where the cottage sits, but they cannot see it or get inside. You're safe."

"Am I safe?" Jawar's bottom lip trembled. Merlin hoisted him half into his lap and hugged him gently, as if he were afraid to cause him any more pain.

"I'm sorry I did not get you out sooner, little prince," Merlin began. "It was not for lack of care, nor effort. But we had to time this perfectly. Your father will be here in less than a few hours. King Castilian's troops have already spotted him outside of their border. I could not retrieve you until the time was right."

"You don't need to apologize," Jawar's eyes fluttered shut. The adrenaline of the escape was beginning to wear off, and his body was so weak that it was only a matter of time before he succumbed to the exhaustion. "Wait, did you say we?"

A gentle hand brushed against his forehead, and for a few seconds, Jawar managed to open his eyes just enough to get a glimpse of her face.

"Hello," Rosa said softly, gently dabbing his face with a warm cloth. "I told you I would get you out."

"Rosa," Jawar struggled to speak.

Her name was the last word that fell from his lips before he slipped into a dreamless sleep. Now was not the time for dreams of fields of wildflowers or visions of his mother singing in the morning light. Jawar did not want to think about anything, and for a moment, he did not want to exist at all. He was merely in a state of unconsciousness, but hopefully, with Merlin's help, he would be strong enough to face their two kingdom's greatest enemy, once and for all.

Chapter 21:

Plan of Peace

Merlin did not know what to expect when Jawar finally managed to escape.

He had hoped that King Castilian would have at least shown him some decency—perhaps not the luxuries he received as the king's ward, but surely being a prince would have gained him some privileges. By the look of Jawar's body, that had been far from the case. His garments hung loosely from his shoulders, his muscles suffering the consequences of weeks of neglect. When he had spoken to the young guard, he had mentioned sneaking him a few meals from the kitchen, but those alone would not have been enough.

"Do you think he'll get through this?" Rosa asked, as they hoisted Jawar's unconscious body onto the thin mattress.

Neo had been standing idly in the kitchen, stirring a pot of his bean soup. He did not know much about healing or taking care of a sick person, but the blacksmith had mentioned that Jawar's stomach would need to get used to full meals again, and soup would be an excellent start. Merlin did appreciate the delicious aroma that filled the cottage and it helped to put them all at ease.

"He's stronger than he looks," Merlin concluded.

"I'm not talking about his physical shape," Rosa corrected herself. "I'm asking if you think he'll be able to overcome all that's happened to him." She pointed her index finger to the side of her head before frowning.

The sorcerer knew what she meant. He just did not know himself. Jawar had always shown great progress in the world of magic, but with the things he endured down in the dungeons, there was no telling what side effects could come of it. They would just have to wait and see. For now, all Merlin could do was help make his body strong again.

"Hand me that vial on the end table. The purple one with the cork," he instructed.

Rosa did as she was told with no questions. She likely knew that it was not the time for a lesson on magic. Their friend was on death's door, and all that mattered was bringing him back.

Uncorking the bottle, Merlin dabbed a few drops of the special brew on the tips of his fingers and rubbed it on Jawar's nose. There was a slight crack of the bone snapping back in place, and the bruising beneath the skin started to heal.

"Healing potion?" Rosa's eyebrow raised slightly. "I should have known."

"It can't heal a stab to the heart, but a broken bone and bruises are easy fixes. There should be a green jar somewhere over there. It looks kind of like a paste. I need that one next, please."

Rosa shifted in the chair that Merlin had purchased for Jawar what seemed like a lifetime ago. Searching through the many different bottles and jars on the end table, she found the one that had been asked for.

"Help me remove his tunic and roll up his trousers as far as you can. This will help to regenerate his muscles. It won't work instantly like the healing potion, but he should soon be able to walk without limping all over the place."

Merlin could have sworn that he saw Rosa's face flush at the thought of taking Jawar's garments off, but she cleared her throat and did it anyway. The sorcerer's heart twinged at the sight of seeing him as nearly flesh and bones. His ribs stuck out as one would expect of someone who had been starved, and his collarbones did too. It had been a long time since Merlin allowed himself to care for another person, and now he knew why. It hurt so much to see them in pain.

The darkness in his soul, while minuscule compared to the pureness of his heart, was on the verge of breaking free again. Jawar did not deserve any of this. But hopefully, their plan would work, and the two kings would see reason. There was no need to go to war over any of this.

Letting out a deep sigh, Merlin stuck his fingers into the paste and gently massaged it all over Jawar's skin. It smelled awful, enough to make Rosa's nose wrinkle in protest, but she did not object or move away. She simply continued to clean Jawar's body of blood and dirt, starting with his hands.

"I'm sure he'll appreciate this once he wakes," Rosa said, breaking the silence. "You should have seen it for yourself. If I had your power, I would have ripped those bars from their hinges and fought every last one of them until he was safe."

Merlin twitched at the insinuation that he had not done all that he could have for Jawar. As much as he wanted to burn down the castle to get his friend out, Merlin had to look at the bigger picture. It was not just Jawar's life that hung in the balance, but all of the people of Taviel and Raimore combined. He was just the piece holding them all together.

Now that King Umar was practically on the castle doorsteps, they might actually have a chance to right the wrongs of the past.

"He's safe now. That's all that matters," Neo said, patting his daughter on the shoulder. "Our work here is done. Let him rest for a few hours. He's going to need it for what's in store today."

The blacksmith was right. But if things did not turn out in the way that Merlin hoped they would, he would not hesitate to use his time-traveling device to take Jawar as far away from this land as possible.

There was no way he was going to let them lock him up again. Not now, not ever.

***

"I think he's starting to wake up."

Merlin slammed his book shut at the sound of Rosa's voice. She had not moved from Jawar's side the entire time he slept. He thought that he heard her speaking to him earlier, but he did his best not to listen. If she had been, he wanted to give her privacy, though it was lacking in his tiny cottage.

"Merlin," Jawar croaked. "Is that you?"

"I'm here," Merlin replied, getting up from his seat and plopping down on the mattress next to his young friend. "How are you feeling?"

"A bit groggy, but I'm sure I'll live." He paused, looking down at himself. They had placed a thin blanket over his body to try to keep him warm, as Merlin did not want to rub off his special paste too soon. It needed to work its way into his body for it to work. "Why do I smell so weird?"

Everyone in the cottage broke out into fits of laughter, Jawar included. The sound alone was like music to his ears.

"Do you think you can sit up?" Neo asked. "There's soup on the fireplace. I thought if you were up for it, you could have a little bowl."

"That sounds wonderful," Jawar smiled. "Thank you."

Neo, pleased to be of some use, scampered about the cottage preparing everyone's meals. Merlin nodded as he took his bowl, and held onto Jawar's as well, but drew the line at spoon-feeding. After a few sips, Jawar's shoulders seemed less tense. He let out a sigh, his eyes fluttered shut for a minute, and Merlin wondered if he was going to fall back into a deep sleep.

"My uncle is responsible for this entire mess," Jawar confessed.

Merlin's heart skipped a beat. "What do you mean?"

Jawar struggled to dig whatever it was he wanted from his pocket. As much as Merlin wanted to intervene, Jawar felt that he needed to push past the pain and do things himself. Otherwise, he might never recover. After a minute of gritting his teeth, Jawar produced a handful of parchments. Some of them had been torn during the fight of his life, and others had unusual stains on them which Merlin did not wish to know about.

"What are they?" Rosa asked.

"Letters. King Castilian came to my cell a few days ago to tell me my fate." Jawar coughed a bit, but cleared his throat and continued. "Apparently, he and my father had been corresponding back and forth for some time now. The letters were not pleasant, to say the very least. He told me that it was the proof he needed to show that I was the traitor he feared. I had no idea why my father would write those things. That's when I realized that he hadn't. It's not his handwriting—it's Hakim's."

"You're certain of this?"

Merlin inspected the letters carefully. The last one proved to be the most insightful. There was something about the words *my brother* that piqued his interest. They were scored, as if the writer had put a great deal of pressure onto the paper when writing it.

"Yes. The only thing I don't know is why he would do this. Why would he willingly put my life in danger? I know we did not have the best relationship, but I figured he at least loved me. He must have known that what he was doing would have severe consequences, and that it would be me who suffered."

Jawar's bottom lip trembled, and a few tears slipped from his eyes. Rosa took it upon herself to curl up into a ball next to Jawar, tucking her head beneath his chin. It looked as if she were the one who needed comfort, but Merlin knew that Jawar likely appreciated the tender gesture more than words could express.

"You know as well as I do that the power of temptation can turn even the greatest of men into beasts," Merlin sighed.

"Well, what are we going to do about it?" Rosa asked. "I can almost guarantee that Jawar's uncle will be riding alongside King Umar into battle. What are we going to do, tell everyone that he wrote the letters and not his father?"

"It sounds easy in practice, but the likelihood of King Castilian believing a word of it is low. He will just assume that we're trying to save Raimore."

"We are," Jawar said, "and Taviel. It's like I have said from the very beginning—I'm the token of truce. The reason I came to Taviel was to keep the peace between our two nations. The only way to do that is by telling the truth and having faith."

"If that's what you want, that's what we'll do," Merlin said. Although deep down, he had about five other plans bouncing around in his head, just in case this one did not work.

"Oh, I almost forgot... Nice job with the charmed key," Jawar smirked. "I lost it, sadly, or I should say gave it away to another one of the prisoners, hoping to cause a massive distraction. It was brilliant."

"Why thank you!" Rosa clapped her hands in delight. "It was all my idea. Merlin was just the one who executed it."

Chapter 22:

Blood Hath Been Shed

"Hakim, where do you think you're going?"

King Umar had stepped outside of his tent just as his brother and three of their generals prepared to mount their horses. He had led Hakim to believe that he was holding the meeting elsewhere when, in truth, it had been in his tent all along. He could not say for certain what exactly his little brother had planned, but he had a gut feeling that it was not going to be good.

"I was just coming to tell you," Hakim huffed. "I left a note in my tent. Some of Taviel's army was spotted in the forest just south of here. We were going to investigate."

King Umar did not buy his lies for a second. "You four were going to go up against a part of Castilian's army?"

"Well, we did not plan to fight them, Your Majesty," Roman, the tallest of the three purred. "We were just going to count numbers, so you could be better prepared."

"There's no need." Umar waved his hand to dismiss them back to their assigned duties. "I already dispatched scouts a few hours ago. I know I said we were going to hunker down and get some rest, but with the Taviel army forming their blockade at the bridge, I think we should head out now."

"What about our troops?" Hakim objected. "They need rest, too. We've been traveling for days. They'll be useless in battle if they cannot hold the weight of their own swords."

"They'll be fine," Umar growled. "Now, do as I say and gather your things. We're leaving within the hour, and I want every last soldier ready to go. That includes you three. I expect your battalions are wandering around the camp wondering what to do with themselves. See to it that they are prepared."

"Yes, King Umar," the three said in unison. Taking one last look at Hakim, the three departed, blending in with the rest of the king's army.

"You know I don't like it when you keep secrets from me." Umar lowered his voice. "Tell me the truth—what are you planning?"

"It's nothing you need to concern yourself with," he groaned. "Let's just focus on getting Jawar back."

As much as Umar wanted to pry the secrets from Hakim's mind, he knew that he did not have the time nor the energy to do so. Besides, he was right—Jawar was their one and only priority, and right now, he was waiting for his father to come to rescue him. Hakim mounted his horse and proceeded to assemble the soldiers under his command.

"Hang in there, Jawar," Umar said to himself. "I'm coming."

***

"Something isn't right," Umar said.

They were nearly to the bridge and the scouts who had first come by said they saw Taviel's army preparing to form a blockade. But there was not a single soul in sight, not one soldier with a flag to offer a surrender, no company to discuss negotiations for both sides to stand down, and no army that they were planning to go up against. Only an empty, barren land lay before them.

"I thought you said Roman had come by here," Umar continued, looking to his brother for an explanation. "I was informed that there would be an army standing between us and the royal city."

"That's what he said," Hakim confirmed. "Perhaps they changed tactics at the last minute."

"Without us noticing?" Umar raised his voice. "I demand to know what's going on right now!"

"Archers!" Raja pointed beneath the bridge.

All at once, an assembly of soldiers marched out from underneath the bridge and pointed their arrows at the first wave of the Raimore army.

"Shields up!" Umar shouted.

The front lines had just barely scrambled to get their shields from their backs as a sea of arrows fell from above. Umar clutched his shield above his head, knowing that his chest plates were thick enough, should a stray arrow come straight for him. It was his head that he was worried about. It was the only piece of his old uniform that refused to fit. He had been but a boy back then, just a few years older than Jawar was now.

Once the initial wave of arrows came to an end, the foot soldiers burst from the reeds by the shoreline. Their battle cry could have been heard for miles. Bucking his horse, Umar did not hesitate to rush into the fight. It was as if that part of him had never left, despite all the years that had gone by.

He wondered if they even deserved peace after all this was said and done. Looking back at it now, he was ashamed to admit that he regretted coming to Taviel with his entire army. They may have lost the battle, but at least his morals would have remained intact. They would be stained forever now. As someone who desperately wanted to establish a new world, one where violence came as a last resort, Umar had done a terrible job of trying to maintain order.

But he could not dwell on the past one second longer. His sword clanged against one of Taviel's soldiers, and then another, and then another. It became difficult to identify who was fighting for which side, as the colors of each kingdom somehow managed to blend together.

Out of nowhere, King Umar was thrown off of his horse, and he landed hard on his back. The wind was knocked from his lungs, and he took in a deep breath, trying to regain his composure. A soldier took it as an opportunity to claim the king's life. Swinging his sword above his head, he prepared to deliver his final blow when a sword pierced through his heart. Looking up, the king spotted Raja, who gave him a quick nod before returning into the horde.

Pushing himself to his feet, the armor threatened to push him back down into the mud, but he managed to keep himself steady. Looking all around, he spotted Hakim with the three generals again. Somehow, they managed to get across the bridge unscathed. Umar waved his hands above his head, trying to get their attention. After about 30 seconds, Hakim finally looked over.

Even though he was a great distance away, Umar swore that he could see betrayal in his eyes. It was as plain as day, and at that very moment, there was not a single thing he could do to prevent it from happening.

"Hakim!" Umar called out. "Don't do this!"

With a final farewell, Hakim removed the crest from his armor and tossed it onto the ground beneath his horse's hooves. In times of war, it was a great dishonor to remove your country's insignia from your uniform. It essentially meant that he had become a rogue soldier.

How could he? Umar thought. My own brother, in our final hour of need, fleeing like a coward.

He watched helplessly as Hakim and the three generals rode off in a southerly direction toward the forest, the place they had claimed to see the army. This had all been a diversion, Umar realized. He had no idea what his brother had planned, but he knew that it had nothing to do with Raimore and Taviel. Worst of all, Hakim did not care about the fate of Umar's son.

**

The first battle against the Taviel army had been a gruesome one.

Many great soldiers lost their lives, on both sides. For Umar, it felt as if it had been over in a matter of minutes. But based on the position of the sun rising on the horizon, he knew it had to have been at least hours. Having only been a small portion of the kingdom's forces, most of the Taviel soldiers had retreated when they realized that they did not have the numbers to fight.

He would have done the same if the roles were reversed, but Umar thought it was cowardly to run from a fight. Perhaps that was just because he was feeling betrayed by his brother's actions.

"Your Majesty," Raja saluted as he approached on foot.

Umar had lost his horse somewhere in the middle of battle, and most of them had run off into the countryside. They would have to walk the rest of the way. It would be a burden on both time and energy, but that was the cost of going to war.

"What is it?" Umar questioned.

"I've done a headcount. We lost 200 men. Fifty are wounded, and it's likely that they won't make it to see the sunset. Thirty have minor injuries and are prepared to fight. The rest went unscathed."

"And Taviel's side?"

"Five hundred dead, sir. No one survived, and those who did fled west. They have likely regrouped with the rest of the army outside of the royal city. That's where we'll face the bulk of them, sir. Just like last time."

"Only now we're fighting to rescue my son's life," Umar pointed out.

When he looked back at all of the reasons that their two nations had gone to war, he never could find a specific reason as to why it happened. The two kings just simply did not get along. It had been that way for centuries, and none of the prior kings had ever felt the need to make a change.

"Do you have a plan, Your Majesty? Now that your second-in-command is missing, you'll have to select—"

"He's not missing," Umar growled. "He did not die in battle with honor. He fled, like a coward. No, it's worse than that, because it's not like he ran because he was scared. He left of his own accord, to fight for his own personal gain. We will not wait for Hakim's return, or the other generals accompanying him. You're second-in-command now, Raja, and I know they are big shoes to fill, but I trust that you will serve Raimore well."

Raja placed a palm over his heart and nodded with gratitude. "I live to serve you and the crown, Your Majesty. Should I die, I hope I go with honor and pride, knowing that it was trying to save Prince Jawar's life."

"Your loyalty will not go unnoticed." Umar placed a single hand on the man's shoulder and squeezed it tightly. "Gather up the troops. We're heading for the city. Whether or not Hakim is already there, I cannot say, but I hope for his sake he's not."

"Right away, Your Majesty," Raja bowed.

Perhaps he misjudged his brother's intentions. There was a chance that he had gone ahead to try to reason with King Castilian. It was a false hope at best, one he was desperately holding on to. He did not want to think of his brother as a traitor. Not when his child's fate hung in the balance.

"Your Majesty," a young soldier squeaked.

Umar turned to find a boy who resembled Jawar so much that it took his breath away. For a second, he forgot everything that was going on in the world. But just as quickly as his mind wandered, it was brought back to reality when the soldier offered him the reins to a new horse.

"We'll be there faster with you leading us on horseback," the soldier said.

"Right. Thank you."

Umar hoisted himself up into the saddle and with one final glance at the army that was congregating near the bridge, clicked his tongue and watched as the soldiers parted to let him pass. Hopefully, there would be nothing else but King Castilian standing in his way.

Chapter 23:

The Power of Excalibur

"Are you sure you want to do this?" Merlin whispered.

Together, the four of them had come up with a plan that Jawar was proud to see through. It did not involve anyone dying, getting locked up, or making unfair sacrifices. For too long, Raimore and Taviel have suffered from a cycle of distaste and distrust. None of it was justifiable. Jawar should know, as he studied both histories. Sure, he had grown up hearing stories from his father about the wars he faced, his father before him, and his father before that. It had always been the same. The tension between the nations would simmer, but all it took was a spark and everything would come crashing down. Last time, Raimore had been the kingdom that suffered the most. It took years to rebuild the country back up to a point of sustainability. The economy suffered, citizens were living on the streets as their homes had been destroyed, and a darkness loomed over the country, one that never truly went away.

The same had been the case for Taviel after the war before that. The number of casualties caused a pit to form in the bottom of Jawar's stomach. Most of those who died were not even soldiers in the army, but just people who got caught in the crossfire.

"It's going to work," Jawar said firmly. "It has to."

"I don't mean to stunt your confidence," Rosa apologized, "but I feel like there's a lot at stake. You're having to put your faith in a king who had you locked up for weeks because he suspected that you were a spy. The second he sees you alive, he may have you executed on the spot."

"Yes, but he also may not. You didn't see the look in his eyes like I did. I know it well, as I've seen it all my life, in my father's eyes. He's not just a king, but a parent. He just wants to protect Prince Darrow. He was afraid that I was sent here to kill his son, and I can't hold that against him."

"You're very noble," Neo acknowledged. "But it's like Merlin said—magic has a mind of its own. If for even a moment you lose focus, there could be catastrophic consequences."

"I know you don't always trust magic, but you have to trust me. I don't know how to explain it, but I just know this is what was meant to happen. As awful as it was rotting away in that dungeon, I needed that to see clarity. My father needed a reason to come to Taviel, so he and King Castilian could stand together as one. The stars have aligned on this blessed day, and we're going to forge a new path, like I have always dreamed of."

Merlin retrieved his most precious belongings from beneath the floorboard. While Jawar could see the sword perfectly well in his hands, he knew that Rosa and Neo could not. With a flick of his wrist, the spell was gone, and the two gasped at the sight.

"So this is it," Neo reached out to touch it, but Merlin swatted his hands away. He scrunched up his nose, feeling offended he was not allowed to touch the magnificent blade.

"It's for your own good," Jawar explained. "Excalibur is cursed, so only those with the blood of the Magi creators can harness its powers."

"That doesn't sound frightening at all." Rosa's eyes widened, and she backed away a few steps.

"I've held it before," Jawar said. Wrapping his hands around the hilt, the sword illuminated for a few seconds, casting the cottage in a soothing light. "See? Not dead."

"Come on," Merlin waved. They gathered in a small circle, each holding someone else's hand, as per the sorcerer's instructions. "We'll be traveling a few seconds into the future for this to work. Picture the shop in your mind. Focus on your senses—the smell, the sounds, the heat against your skin. Hold onto that and we should be fine."

"Should?" Rosa opened one eye and glared at Merlin. "We're putting a lot of faith in maybe's and should's."

"Close your eyes and focus. I'm going to count down from three. Ready?" Jawar squeezed Merlin's hand as tightly as he could. This was it. There was no turning back now, even if he wanted to. "Three, two, one."

***

Jawar barely had a chance to breathe before they were zapped into the basement of the blacksmith's shop.

He quickly opened his eyes and was relieved to see Excalibur in his hand, and that everyone had made it there in one piece. Rosa touched the top of her head and her arms, as if she were afraid that part of herself would be missing. Neo stumbled a little bit, struggling to regain his composure. Merlin had said that was a typical side effect of time traveling. It was different for everyone.

The vibration of the war horns made Jawar's skin crawl. He feared that they had come too late. Scrambling up the narrow staircase and reaching the main level of the blacksmith's shop, he peered out of the front window. They were in the perfect line of sight to see King Castilian upon a white steed with hundreds of soldiers surrounding him in the courtyard. The only person not accounted for was Prince Darrow. Jawar assumed that he was tucked safely inside the castle with his younger brother and mother.

The soldiers parted as King Umar marched into view. His army went on for miles, but by his side, were those carrying the banners of Raimore.

Besides the two opposing sides, the marketplace and courtyard were completely empty. He had no idea where all the people were. They were probably hiding just as they were, trying to catch a glimpse of what was to come.

"He looks just like you," Rosa whispered.

Jawar could not help but smile at that, but he quickly shook his head, knowing that now was not the time to be melting at compliments.

"King Castilian!" King Umar's voice shook the windows of the blacksmith's shop. "I had hoped that we could have been more civilized than this, but you left me with no other choice. Release my son and I will bring you no further harm. Refuse me, and I will tear your castle apart, brick by brick."

The King of Taviel looked unphased on the outside, but Jawar knew that watching the kingdom fall was the last thing he wanted to do. "Even if I could hand over the little prince, I wouldn't. He's a traitor, like you, and broke the truce we had signed together."

"If you could?" Umar questioned. "Do you mean to tell me you don't have my son bound in chains in the depths of your dungeons?"

King Castilian hesitated, as if choosing his next words wisely. "He was, but he is no longer. Last night he escaped, freeing several other prisoners in the process. He fled into the forest, and he has not been seen since."

"If you killed—"

"Jawar, you have to do something," Merlin nudged him out of his state of panic. "This is what you were born to do."

Trying his best to stop from shaking, he gripped the hilt of Excalibur with both hands, mostly because he was afraid that he would drop the thing before he made it to the center of the courtyard.

"I need you all to stay inside," Jawar instructed. "I'm not exactly sure what kind of power will be unleashed, and I'd rather you be safe than sorry."

"No way," Merlin refused. "You're not going out there alone."

"I won't be alone," Jawar said. "We're kindred spirits, remember? You can feel my magic just as much as I can feel yours."

A flicker of sadness glimmered in Merlin's eyes, but he did not protest. This was not his fight, and he knew that as much as the others did.

"Just don't get yourself killed," the sorcerer warned. "Or I'll bring you back and kill you myself."

Jawar smirked, and with that, he slipped out of the blacksmith's shop just as his friends took cover behind the forge.

Luckily, no one seemed to be paying any attention to him. The tension in the courtyard made the hairs on the back of Jawar's neck rise. Just as his father was about to dismount from his horse and demand a duel, Jawar ran to the centre of the courtyard as fast as he could.

Standing between the two kings, he held Excalibur above his head and plunged it into the dirt at his feet. "Enough!"

A massive explosion erupted from the tip of the blade. The shockwave sent both Umar and Castilian flying backward, along with dozens of the soldiers standing within the vicinity. Windows exploded, including those of the blacksmith's shop. When the magic dissipated, Jawar's hands were stained black, but thankfully, it had not been the deadly curse. The ground was burnt, tiny little flames charred the grass, and Jawar was quick to stomp them out.

"Jawar?" Umar struggled to sit up from the weight of his armor. "You're alive!"

"Seize him!" Castilian pointed.

"Wait!" Jawar wielded Excalibur once more, and everyone halted. "This is the cursed blade, and I don't want to use it again, but I will if we cannot maintain order. You both need to know the truth, the whole truth, and then you can decide if the truce can be restored." Sucking in a deep breath, the two kings nodded, and Jawar continued. "There is a traitor in Raimore, but it is not I. King Umar never wrote the letters you received." He looked at King Castilian, holding up the crumbled parchments in his hands. "And Father, I can only assume the ones you read were not from Castilian, either. Hakim is a traitor. He's the one behind all the lies and deceit. He wrote these letters, he brought me here, and he doesn't want Taviel and Raimore to establish peace."

"How can you expect me to believe a single word coming from your mouth?" King Castilian narrowed his eyes in disbelief.

Jawar smiled and held up his right hand. On his middle finger, he wore a vibrant blue ring, and it glowed as if there were a tiny flame inside. "You'll find it rather easy, Your Majesty. This here is the Ring of Truth. For as long as I shall wear it, I cannot tell a lie."

Chapter 24:

The Disease of Power

"For as long as I shall wear it, I cannot tell a lie."

Merlin had heard only the last few words of Prince Jawar's declaration as he emerged from the shattered windows of the blacksmith shop. Neo and Rosa lingered just a few paces behind him, still a bit shaken by the sheer force of Excalibur. Despite the circumstances they currently found themselves in, Merlin could not help but shine with a sense of pride. When he had first met Jawar, he had no idea the kind of power he held deep inside. Now, he was harnessing that magic, and for a noble purpose.

The tension was still sizzling between the two kings, but it was not nearly as deadly as before. Merlin assumed that they were both just trying to wrap their minds around the truth, having believed a lie for so long.

"I apologize, King Castilian," Merlin confessed. "It was I who broke Prince Jawar out of your dungeon, but I felt it was necessary. We needed you to see reason, but we couldn't do that with him behind bars."

King Castilian walked toward Merlin and Jawar, as did King Umar. Merlin, feeling a sense of guardianship over the little prince, took a generous step in front of him, using his body as a shield.

"Can I see the letters, please?" Umar requested.

Jawar, without saying a word, handed them over to his father. Merlin noticed that there were tears in his eyes, likely from the overwhelming joy of seeing his family after having suffered for so long. Umar scanned the letters briefly, his eyebrows pinching together as he flipped through each one.

"Not a single one of these are from me," Umar confirmed. "They bear my seal, yes, but this is not my handwriting. See here." Walking back to his horse, he retrieved a scroll from one of the pouches and held it up next to the last letter. "Do you see the difference? While my handwriting has flourishes on most of the letters, these here are bolder, and the letters are further apart."

King Castilian's face turned beet red. Who would have thought that just a single mix-up of letters would do so much harm? In all honesty, Merlin had witnessed great empires fall over something as menial as this.

"It just doesn't make any sense." Castilian scratched the top of his head. "Who would do something like this? Why would they want to see us tear each other apart?"

"It's Hakim," Jawar stated. "I know it in my heart to be true."

"Indeed, I do fear my little brother was behind all this. The more I think about it, the more I see the truth behind the lies. He had been the one to suggest that Jawar come to Taviel and live as your ward, he offered to remain in Raimore over the last few months and handle some of my political affairs as I worked on establishing order in the kingdom, and it was he who said that you had declared war against our nation. Looking around now, I can see that you were not as prepared as he had led me to believe."

He was correct. While the last two weeks that Jawar had been imprisoned had been a scramble to gather as many able-bodied men as possible, Taviel's army was easily outnumbered by Raimore's by at least 3-1. If they had fought, there was no doubt in Merlin's mind that King Umar would have come out on top.

"I feel like such a fool," King Castilian sighed. "If only I had believed Jawar when he said that he had no part in all of this, perhaps we could have saved countless lives and wasted resources."

"I think the better thing to ask is why Hakim went through all of this trouble to divide the two kingdoms in the first place," Merlin interrupted. "Surely, it has something to do with a power struggle, but I've never seen a man go to such drastic lengths so that he could have himself a crown."

"That's a good question indeed, sorcerer."

The four of them followed the voice to find a man who looked a lot like the king emerging from the courtyard gate. Three soldiers rode on his left, while dozens of others trailed behind, some on foot, and some on horseback.

"Let me guess, that's your uncle." Merlin whispered to Jawar, who, unable to speak at the moment, merely nodded.

"Hakim!" Umar gasped. "Jawar tells me that you forged these letters to make it look like I was the one who wrote them. You made me believe that King Castilian was set to kill my son and start a war, but you were behind it all. Why?"

"If you really have to ask yourself that, you're not a very wise king," Hakim smirked. "It all comes down to power, doesn't it? That's why our two families have always fought. To establish dominance over the other. It is why mankind has feuded for centuries. We all crave one thing and one thing only. Power."

"You're wrong!" Jawar shouted, pointing the tip of Excalibur at his uncle. "Some of us just want to live in a world where peace exists. I'd give up the throne if it came down to it."

Hakim's eyes glowed at the sight of Excalibur. Suddenly, Merlin had pieced it all together. He was not here for his brother's throne, or Castilian's for that matter. He was here because of him, and for the sword.

Placing a hand on Jawar's forearm, he nudged him to lower the blade before standing in front of both Castilian and Umar. He was not afraid to face this man—in fact, he was more than willing to put him in his place if he needed to.

"How did you know I was a sorcerer?" Merlin tilted his head to the side. It was a simple question, but he sensed the uneasiness seeping from Hakim's pores. He thought he had the high ground, and the element of surprise, but it would take a lot more than a mortal and lust for complete and utter domination to catch him off guard.

Leaping off of his horse, Hakim withdrew something from around his neck. Narrowing his eyes, Merlin recognized the device instantly. "Stand back," he shoved Jawar a little too much, but he managed to catch himself before he fell. "That's a siphoner."

"That's right," Hakim grinned. "All I need is to get close enough to drain his magic. Perhaps I can take yours too, nephew."

"You go anywhere near my son, and I'll cut you down, brother," Umar growled. He unsheathed his sword, and surprisingly, so did King Castilian. Forming a united front, Jawar's uncle did not stand a chance.

"This is between you and me, Merlin. Or are you going to have them fight your battles for you?"

Holding his hand out, Merlin hurled a ball of magic just over Hakim's shoulder. The second it connected with one of his general's chest, it burst, sending the man flying through the air.

"Surrender now," Merlin began, the magic seeping out of his fingertips, ready to strike at a moment's notice. "While I'm still feeling generous."

With a snap of his fingers, his two other generals fired arrows at Merlin, but they were easy to dodge. However, while distracted, Hakim closed the gap between them, holding his device as high as he could. The magic circling his hands was siphoned, and Merlin felt the effects almost immediately. If he were not capable, he might lose every last drop of his powers.

"Go ahead, sorcerer," Hakim hissed. "Do your worst."

Unexpectedly, Jawar charged at his uncle. Holding Excalibur with both hands, Hakim waved his hand in the air once more, and two arrows whipped through the air, heading straight for the young prince. Merlin tackled Jawar to the side, somewhat crushing him in the process. The sword fell just a few feet out of reach, and Hakim had his sights set on it. Merlin tried to crawl for it, but that was when he realized that Hakim intended to get rid of his nephew, once and for all.

Cursing under his breath, Merlin picked Excalibur up using a levitation spell and drove the blade straight through Hakim's chest. He fell to his knees instantly, and after a few beats, he coughed, and blood splattered the ground in front of him.

Jawar grabbed onto the hilt as his uncle fell backward, the sword releasing from his chest. Just like that, Hakim was dead. Everyone in the courtyard froze. Merlin had done one of the few things he had promised himself that he never would.

"I'm so sorry," he said, pulling Jawar into a hug, trying to get him to look away. When Jawar wrapped his arms around Merlin's waist, he sighed with relief, fearing that the little prince would hate him forever for what he had done.

"You saved me. He was never going to stop until he got what he wanted."

It was the truth—that was the disease of power—it blinds to the point that all sight of honor and dignity are lost.

Chapter 25:

Feast for Peace

It had been two weeks since Merlin saved Jawar's life.

A lot had happened during that time. The first, and perhaps most important in Jawar's eyes, was that Merlin had taken Excalibur back to his cottage and hidden it with all the rest of the artifacts, including the ring that he had used to tell the truth. Hakim had made it clear that it was not just dangerous sorcerers from a different time who wanted the sword for its power, but people in this realm too. Merlin had assured Jawar that no one would be able to find it. They would need to kill him first for the spell to wear off, and he promised that was never going to happen.

The second thing that happened was King Umar, his father, returned to Raimore with what remained of his army. He had said that he was going to dismiss the army, where any of the veterans would be compensated for their services over the years and also declared war heroes. The same would be given to the newest recruits that Hakim had conscripted (without Umar's consent) but they would be assigned new positions in the royal guard. They would protect their nation from themselves, as there would always be crime, no matter how much they fought for peace. All that really mattered was that the alliance between Taviel and Raimore still held strong.

While the two weeks in the dungeons had felt like months, or even years in Jawar's eyes, the two waiting for his father and mother to return to Taviel came and went in the blink of an eye. To be fair, he had kept himself rather busy. He not only helped Neo and Rosa restore the blacksmith's shop so they could get it up and running again, but King Castilian had also taken him under his wing. He and Prince Darrow resumed their tutoring in the morning, and when the evening rolled around, Jawar was free to venture to Merlin's cottage.

He had established a bit of a routine now in Taviel, one that he was evidently benefitting from.

Tonight, King Castilian and Queen Kenna were holding a grand feast in the great hall, with the Al Naseem's as their honored guests. Normally, events like these were prohibited for commoners, and only royal members of either kingdom were permitted to attend. However, Jawar had made it clear from the start that there were to be a few exceptions to that rule. He had eagerly sent a formal invitation to Rosa and Neo, asking them if they would attend in his honor. He even offered to pay for a new dress, if that was something Rosa had wanted. Despite Neo's objections saying that it was not necessary, and that they had plenty of garments to choose from, Rosa had dragged Jawar around the marketplace for an entire afternoon. She had purchased half a dozen gowns, claiming that she wanted to have options. He did not protest, but if he were being honest, she could show up in the apron she wore at the shop for all he cared. Jawar just wanted his friends there to celebrate with him.

That meant that Merlin was also invited to attend. As usual, he acted as if he were above the whole concept of balls, feasts, and grand parties, but agreed to accompany Jawar, stating he would hate for him to be the only magic wielder in the room.

"Do you really think it's just the two of us?" Jawar had asked one afternoon as they sat on the front porch of Merlin's cottage.

It had been a beautiful sunny day, and the forest had come alive with woodland creatures running about the underbrush in search of food.

"Honestly? No, I don't. Magic, while rare, always has a way of revealing itself. Look at yourself. You had no idea you were a sorcerer until a few months ago. The same could be said for others. All it takes is a little cohesion and that part of them will be reborn."

"We should try to find them," Jawar had suggested. "Kind of like the artifacts. It shouldn't be that hard. You and I can feel each other's magic, and we might be able to feel others too."

"We'll see," Merlin sighed. "Sometimes people don't want you to know that they can wield magic. It's a choice, one neither you nor I can make for them."

Jawar had left the conversation at that. He knew there was more to it than that, and Merlin that was holding back, but he figured he would explain it all when at the right time. For now, he was content with it just being the two of them.

***

The steady beat of drums had Jawar flinging himself at his window. The flags and banners of Raimore flapped in the wind as the king's procession made its way through the marketplace. Many of the shop owners had come out onto the pedestrian path to wave at the assembly of carriages as they passed. Jawar spotted Rosa and Neo from a distance. Rosa's colorful hair ribbons were hard to miss, even in a crowd of hundreds of people.

"Your Grace." One of the servants knocked on Jawar's door before letting herself in. "Do you need help getting dressed for the feast?"

"No," Jawar giggled. "I've been ready for hours. Is King Castilian downstairs already?"

"Yes. He and the queen are waiting for your parents. They'll be arriving any moment. If you're quick, you should beat them to the courtyard!"

Bouncing up and down like a jack rabbit, Jawar twirled past the servant, flashing her a toothy smile on his way out. He nearly plowed over Prince Darrow as he raced out into the hall.

"I'm so sorry!" Jawar cringed. "I didn't see you."

Luckily, Prince Darrow did not look that bothered, even though he almost collided with a stone wall. "It's fine. I'd be this excited too if I hadn't seen my mother in months."

"Shall we?" Jawar waved his hand toward the stairwell, a subtle gesture to challenge the prince to a race.

The two laughed as they raced the entire way down and were very much out of breath by the time that they made it out to the courtyard.

"There you two are," Queen Keena commented. "I thought you were going to miss it."

Standing in between his two guardians, Jawar had a flashback of when he and his parents had greeted Hakim and his cousins. That had been the day that his life changed forever. While there had been a few bumps along the road, a couple of misunderstandings, and some near-death experiences, overall, Jawar would not have changed it for the world.

It was as Merlin pointed out during their first adventure hunting down artifacts—every single person's destiny has already been predestined. Fate works in mysterious ways, and there is nothing that we can do to change it. If Jawar was meant to perish by his uncle's hand, then one way or the other, it would have happened. That was not to say that they all did not have a purpose, or that they should never try to figure out what it is, but there are greater forces at work. It was perfectly fine to not know every aspect of one's life.

One of the five carriages parked right in front of the main doors of the castle. Jacia, Jawar's mother, burst through the doors as soon as it came to a stop. Tears streamed down her cheeks, and Jawar leaped into her arms, hugging her as tightly as he possibly could.

"Oh, my son," she cried, burying her face into the crook of his neck. "I've missed you like the moon misses the stars when the sun comes out.

"Mother," Jawar complained, his cheeks burning hot from embarrassment. "It hasn't been that long."

She released her death grip and readjusted her dress, making sure that she looked all well and proper. Dabbing underneath her eyes with a piece of cloth, she smiled, cupping his face with both hands. "No, I suppose you're right. But when you left Raimore, you were my little boy, and now you've grown up practically overnight."

"It's probably from all that time he spends in the blacksmith's shop," Queen Keena winked. "He goes there nearly every afternoon."

"Oh?" His mother inquired. "This wouldn't happen to have anything to do with a young lady now, would it?"

"Mother!"

"Enough teasing, darling." King Umar placed his hand around his wife's waist and held her tightly. "Or I fear our son might melt into a puddle."

"Oh, speaking of the young lady," Queen Keena beamed. "Here come Rosa and Neo now."

"Wonderful!" Jacia clapped. Turning on her heels, she searched the crowd until Jawar reluctantly pointed them out.

Rosa, confident as she always was, curtsied in front of Queen Jacia and King Umar, before offering each of the two queens a single rose. "Your Majesties, I was told once that it was a nice gesture to bring a small gift to the hosts. I know it's not much, but—"

"It's beautiful," Jacia assured her. "That's very kind of you."

"Yes," Keena agreed. "You're a thoughtful young lady."

"Queen Jacia, King Umar, this is my father, Neo. He runs the blacksmith shop here in the royal city. He makes the finest swords you'll ever use."

"Oh, Rosa," Neo waved his hands, trying his best to be humble. "I'm sure that weapons are the last things on their minds right now."

Merlin appeared in a puff of smoke, scaring nearly everyone half to death—everyone except Jawar, as he had sensed his arrival down to the very second.

"Apologies," he grinned. "Didn't mean to startle you. I'm not late, am I?"

"Right on time," King Castilian informed. "Let's all go inside, shall we? The chefs have been working tirelessly for days preparing this feast for us all. I'd hate to see it go cold because we were too busy chatting outside."

They followed behind His Majesty, who led them straight to the great hall. Along the way, he pointed out different wings of the castle, informing the servants where they could put Queen Jacia and King Umar's belongings, as they were going to be staying for a few days before returning home.

"How are Tierra and Usha?" Jawar asked his mother as they sat down at their table. "I miss them both terribly."

"They've come with us," she smiled. "You'll get a chance to see them after the feast."

Jawar deflated a bit. He wished that he had known sooner that they were coming. He would have asked King Castilian if they could have attended the feast as well. Merlin planted himself next to Jawar, while Neo and Rosa sat across from them both. Servants came around almost immediately and started plating their first course.

The soup smelled delicious, and Merlin helped himself to a few pieces of bread from the center of the table, not caring for the conversation.

"It's not Neo's famous bean stew, but it'll do," Jawar joked as he ate a spoonful.

After a few minutes of eating and hushed conversation, King Castilian stood up from his seat and clicked the side of his goblet. The room fell to silence, and Jawar glanced at Merlin, curious as to what the fuss was all about.

"Thank you all for your attention. I just wanted to say how grateful Keena and I are that you could all attend our feast this evening. Tonight, we are hosting it in honor of Prince Jawar of Raimore," he paused momentarily, allowing the guests to applaud before proceeding. "Without his courage and determination to cast light on the truth and convince us that we're not so different, I don't believe that any of us would be sitting here tonight. He has taken his responsibility as the token of truce between our two nations seriously, and for that, we are indebted to him. Please, raise your cups in gratitude to my beloved ward!"

Jawar wanted nothing more than to slip beneath the table and disappear, hating that so many people were looking at him. Merlin placed his arm on the back of his chair and gently squeezed his neck, relieving some of the tension in his body.

"Don't worry. Once the second course comes out, they'll forget all about you."

"Thanks," Jawar chuckled.

King Castilian and Queen Keena made their way over to their table, with Jawar's father not far behind. "Jawar," he whispered, "might we have a word with you?"

Swallowing a lump in his throat, Jawar nodded. He proceeded to follow the two kings out into the hallway, where they could speak more privately. "Did I do something wrong?" Jawar asked. "Was I supposed to make a speech? I can go back inside and—"

"You've done nothing wrong, son." Umar placed his arm around his son and hugged him close. "We wanted to ask you about your duties as the peacekeeper. Castilian and I both agreed that you have fulfilled your role, and that it is not necessary to continue living in Taviel, if you don't want to."

"What?" Jawar blinked. Out of everything they could have said, Jawar never would have expected that. "Do you not want me here anymore?"

"No, it's not that!" King Castilian reassured him. "We just know that Raimore is your home, and I know you may have felt as if it was a bit of an obligation to stay despite what happened, but we wanted to tell you that we are relieving you from your duties."

Jawar gnawed at the inside of his cheek. He thought about everything that had happened over the last few months. While it had not been all good, it had not been all bad either. He had formed friends and bonds with people who he was just not ready to say goodbye to.

Besides, there was so much he had yet to learn about his magic from Merlin, and there was no way he would be able to do it all on his own.

"I appreciate you taking into consideration what I want, but," he inhaled a deep breath and looked his father in the eye, "I don't think—no, I know I'm not ready to leave Taviel yet. I hope you understand."

King Umar nodded, but there was still a flicker of pain in his eyes, as if he knew that he was going to have to depart from his son once more. "You're forging your own path in life. How can I stand in the way of that? Just know that you can come home to visit us any time, and I pray that you do, for your mother's sake."

Jawar and King Umar embraced before the king kissed his son on the top of his head. "I will, Father, I promise."